Escape

The Liana Brooks Sci Fi Collection

LIANA BROOKS

OTHER WORKS

Find other works by the author at www.lianabrooks.com.

ESCAPE

THE LIANA BROOKS SCI FI COLLECTION

Liana Brooks

AUSTRALIA

Print ISBN: 978-1-922434-49-4
eBook ISBN: 9798201113728

www.inkprintpress.com

National Library of Australia Cataloguing-in-Publication Data
Brooks, Liana 1982—
Escape: The Liana Brooks Sci Fi Collection
140 p.   cm.
ISBN: 978-1-922434-49-4
Inkprint Press, Canberra, Australia
1. Fiction—Science Fiction—Collections & Anthologies 2. Fiction—Science Fiction—Genetic Engineering 3. Fiction—Science Fiction—Space Opera 4. Fiction—Short Stories

Summary: Nine sci fi stories offering escape from the ordinary.

First Edition: May 2022

Cover design © Inkprint Press.

These stories are for anyone who wants to run away from it all.

CONTENTS

FOREWORD

Short stories are strange and wily beasts. At least for me. Perfect short stories distill the essence of the universe into a few perfect lines of prose and leave you thinking of them long after The End. I don't think I've ever achieved a perfect short story. What I hope I have managed to do in this collection is viciously contain the idea of escape in under 100,000 words.

Ursula K. LeGuin paraphrased J.R.R. Tolkien saying, "Fantasy is escapist, and that is its glory. If a soldier is imprisoned by the enemy, don't we consider it his duty to escape? ... If we value the freedom of mind and soul, if we're partisans of liberty, then it's our plain duty to escape, and to take as many people with us as we can!"

Each of these science fiction stories is a teeny-tiny escape hatch from a reality. A chance to run away from all your worries, if only for a moment. A chance to explore somewhere else, even if the time spent is fleeting. The stories come from all over. From idle thoughts as I hung up laundry on a hot summer day and from the depths of postpartum depression as I sat in a lovely house, in a lovely town, in a lovely life and felt trapped by despair. Some of these short stories were originally mean to be part of a larger novel. Others were quick explorations of emotions. They are all a momentary escape from the ordinary and I hope they are the exit you're looking for.

NEON SNOW

SNOW FELL IN LARGE, FLUFFY FLAKES THROUGH THE night, drifting between the multicolored Christmas lights and the palm fronds at the edge of the Junkyard. Yes, snow when it was eighty degrees out with ninety-nine percent humidity. It was better to think of it as snow than chemical ash from the permastorm that churned over the Gulf of Mexico, spitting hurricanes up and down the Atlantic seaboard.

Don't lick it. Don't touch it. Don't—for the love of all the gods—try to melt the stuff. Let it fall. Sweep it away. Dump it somewhere far from civilization, or at least far from the bits of civilization that have money to pay to get the snow far away from them.

Yalana breathed in, taking in the smell of rancid garbage rotting along the dark street, the brine of the ocean air lapping against the beach, the smoke and spice of the Junkyard. It wasn't as sterile as a city building, nor fetid as the alleys where work sometimes called her. It smelled of death—everything on Earth did these days—but it was a lively, irreverent death that flipped the bird to the satellites overhead and the lunar colonies watching everyone down here who was still waiting for rescue.

A flake of snow came uncomfortably close to her face. Yalana blew it away, hunched her shoulders, and flipped the collar of her camel-colored coat up. Long sleeves, long pants in a darker brown, heavy brown combat boots hidden under the slacks. With a little luck, the only thing she'd burn tonight was time and the goodwill of the coast guard commander, who was probably just realizing that she hadn't left the port to cruise around the open water with her lover.

The Junkyard was under quarantine; it had been most her life. It was one of those festering sores of modern living that polite society liked to forget existed. A little town on the Florida panhandle that had continually voted to tax the poor rather than the rich and support land grabs over addressing the rising sea levels.

The rich left when the tide got high. Everyone else, the ones who thought they were one lucky break away from being rich enough to leave, were either dead or somewhere in this half-floating park of madness.

Houses on stilts and houseboats were tied together by weak ropes and anchored to the pieces of mud the storms hadn't yet washed away. It was only a matter of time before the Junkyard was another set of flotsam battering the sea walls protecting Tallahassee.

The people here didn't care.

They came because they didn't want to go to rehab for whatever vice they loved so much. Or maybe because they'd stopped loving everything and wanted to die in a party.

Music and uneasy laughter rolled out of the windows. Everything was for sale in the Junkyard. Everyone had a price.

It was a good place to get lost.

And a good place to hunt for lost souls.

The mud path from the port had once been lined with wood, but most of it had washed away. Now the land underfoot was changing, growing dryer with each step, rising upwards into a small hillock crowned by chain link fences with wood and steel debris lashed to them.

Fist-sized lightbulbs in every color imaginable were strung along the top of the fence, dancing gently in the tropical air.

Two large sections of gate were propped open by heavy barrels of burning driftwood. Blue and purple flames crawled skyward, singeing the snow and giving off a choking smoke that caught the light in odd ways.

A man stepped out of the shadows, wiping large hands on a dirty, yellow cloth. He wore a ripped black vest and faded, gray pants too large for him, held up by a heavy black belt. His eyes were dark and far more focused than any Junkyard denizen was expected to be.

He cocked his head, the light filling in more colors. Purple hair tied up in a knot—and just the knot; the rest of his head was shaved. The rest of him looked hairless too, probably a sign of snow poisoning. It leeched in like that, slowly killing off the outer layers of the body until the skin was little more than scar tissue. In the city it was treatable. Out here...

...She'd worn a coat for a reason.

"You look like you're a long way from home," the man said in a low drawl with hints of New Orleans and Atlanta.

"I am." Yalana put her bare hands in her pockets. "Ever heard of Quebec? It's north of here."

The man's eyebrows—what was left of them—went up and fell with little sign of recognition. "North is as far as the moon."

"Hmm. Well then. You know north where the Yankees live? I was born north of that north."

"I know about Canada." He smirked. "What I don't know is what a pretty little snow bunny is doing playing down here with the sharks." He turned and his vest opened enough to show the black ink outline of a shark with tribal knots.

"Since when was this Shark territory? Word was this belonged to Shiftly."

The man shook his head. "Sorry, beautiful. Shiftly's shuffled off."

Dead. Two-week-old intel was the best money could buy and it still wasn't enough.

"You looking for trouble in general?" the man asked. "Or just the kind Shiftly sold?"

"I'm looking for something special." It was doubtful the man could see her smile in the dark, and even less likely that he'd understand why she was smiling, but she smiled anyway.

"Special costs extra." He made a point to turn and look her up and down. "You got money. We like money here."

"I'll pay with anything but my body. The rest"—she opened her arms—"you can have it. I'll walk out of here naked if it gets me what I want."

He sauntered closer. In the firelight his face was carved and hard. Dangerous. Lethal. "What is so special you're risking your skin for it, beautiful?"

"My lover." She pulled the picture of grinning man from her pocket. In the photo he still had youthful, chubby cheeks, even if his fair hair was receding. "I'll pay anything to get him back."

"Anything?" The man with the purple hair and the shark on his side took the picture. "For him?"

"Yes."

For a minute the Junkyard dog didn't seem like he believed her. "His life means that much to you?"

"It means everything to me."

"You'd give up everything for him?"

"Except my own life. Yes. My body isn't for sale."

The man turned the photograph over in his hands.

Snow fell silently between them.

Yalana's lips twitched up in a cold smile. "You've seen him."

The man shrugged in acknowledgment. "This man. Beautiful, you don't want him."

"I do."

"He's..." The man shook his head. "His head's not right."

"I want him for his body, not his brain."

That earned her a skeptical look. "His body?"

"Yes."

The man turned, fully displaying hard muscles and island-tanned skin. Whether he'd been born with dark gold skin or simply spent too much time in the sun was impossible to tell in this light. His features were an amalgam of every nation that had fought over this blood-soaked sand bar in the past seven centuries. "You're hurting my ego, beautiful."

"I'm sure your ego will survive the night."

He tapped the photograph again. "I know how you can find him."

"Name the price."

"No haggling?"

"I don't need to haggle. I can pay or I can walk."

The man's smile chilled the hot night air. "Give me his last kiss."

"You want to kiss Jackson? Fine."

The man shook his head. "No, not the last kiss from him. The last kiss for him, from you. I want the kiss you want to give your lover before he dies."

The intel hadn't included anything about kissing. It was right on the border of her comfort zone, but not an impossible line to cross, merely unpleasant. She'd suffered through much worse over the years.

"Isn't your lover worth a kiss?"

"Are you clean?" Yalana asked.

"Clean as a whistle," the man promised.

"Clean as a whistle on the sand of a dirty playground covered in snow." There were antibiotic shots on the boat though. It would probably be enough. "Fine. I kiss you and you give me Jackson."

"Ah. No. You give me your last kiss for this man. One final kiss for your love, and then you may never, ever kiss him again."

The tension in her shoulders eased. "If I do?"

"He'll die," the man said simply.

"You'll watch? You'll know? That seems unlikely."

The man shrugged. "Call it superstition."

"Whatever. A kiss for Jackson. That's the trade. No touching. No extras. Just mouths. No blood."

"Come here." His voice was seductive.

She raised an eyebrow. "The trade is for a kiss. I won't come when you call. You want payment, come here." She put her hands back in her pockets, fingers stroking the smooth handle of her gun.

"You are a very angry kitten." He stepped toward her, hands held out to either side but not reaching for her.

Yalana kept her expression bored. If the man was looking for a reaction from her, he wasn't going to get one.

He was larger up close. Taller. Broader. Far more captivating. "It has to be a real kiss," he warned. "I'll know if you're thinking of your lover or not."

"You're a mind reader now?" She almost smiled for real.

"I have many talents."

"Prove it." She closed her eyes and focused, not on Jackson, but on the dream of love. Moonlight on water. A house in the swamps surrounded by water and lightning bugs. Laughter. Her lover's lips on her neck. Warm arms embracing her.

Lips—real lips—touched hers, soft and commanding. For a moment she was in the dream, the smell of wood smoke and her lover's soap curling around her. A tongue stroking hers, promising a night filled with delights.

A kiss that left her glowing with anticipation was replaced by a cold absence.

She opened her eyes and found herself face to face with the stranger.

Dark eyes held hers, emotions flashing like strange fish through stormy seas. "You'll never have that with Jackson again. Never. If you kiss him, if you try to take back what you gave, his life is forfeit."

"I kiss you and get the magic kiss of death?" Yalana raised an eyebrow. "Don't promise me things like that. I might become a repeat client."

"I know what you felt. Your dream of a house in the quiet, under a clear sky."

"Keep talking like that and you're going to have recruiters knocking on your door. The military loves people who are more than what they seem."

The man smirked. "I don't take orders from anyone."

"Then we have something in common." And she'd won the first round. "How do I find Jackson?"

"You'll have to follow me." Round two to the stranger. He turned away quietly, walking through the gates towards a log house on stilts with the same garbage patch decoration as the fence.

Yalana studied it and shook her head. "What did you do, paint the house with glue before the last hurricane and catch whatever came your way?"

"It helps," the man said.

Helped with what, was the question. But not one she had time to pay for. If she wasn't back to the dock before dawn, she'd have larger problems than the ones already threatening to destroy everything around her.

The house was dark. Not a surprise. The Junkyard wasn't exactly on any city's grid. Glass hurricane lamps with oil sat on windowsills unlit. The lanterns outside gave an illusion of light, but not enough to see more than ominous shadows.

"Here." The man stopped in the middle of the darkness. There was a scratching sound, glass against wood, and then a small orb of glowing blue liquid was shoved towards her. "Not as good as the surveillance in a city, but it will glow brighter as you get closer to him."

Yalana shook it, watching the liquid inside as it jumped and swirled. "Interesting. What's it made out of?"

"Stuff."

"What happens if I break the bottle?"

"Don't."

"Worried about losing a lucrative trade secret?"

"Worried the stuff smells like rancid potatoes and it burns your eyes worse than snow. And it evaporates fast. Breaking the bottle isn't worth your time. Remember what happens to curious kittens."

"Curiosity killed the cat, but ingenuity brought it back."

"That's not how the saying goes."

It was for her. "If I can't find Jackson, I'll be back."

"You want your kiss back?"

"No. I'll take repayment in blood. Kitty cats eat fish, didn't you know?"

Leaving the building was easy, all she did was follow the light. By the time she reached what was laughably called the town square, the orb in her hand was glowing brightly enough to illuminate the muddy path in front of her.

She tested it, walking east and then west, watching the glow to see if it was actually reacting to her movements or only growing because the chemicals inside the glass were growing brighter.

It glowed brightest as she walked north by north-east, toward the smell of smoke and the sound of drums.

People fell out of the shadows, approaching her and then veering away when they saw the orb. The Shark Man must have had more influence than he let on.

Bottles. Glass. Chemicals. Sobriety.

He was probably supplying drugs of one kind or another. Medicine was expensive, even if a person had a city job. Here in the Junkyard there would be no state-funded medical supplies. The man wouldn't be the first to leave a life of rigid laws to enjoy the hedonistic pleasures that medical skills could bring.

He'd demanded a kiss from her just for a bottle. What was he asking from others?

The thought twisted her gut. *Should have shot him when I had the chance.* Predators like that could never be reformed.

An overly thin woman wearing a ripped, green dress and lanky hair with snow burns broke away from the nearest cluster of community to approach Yalana. "Who are you?"

"I'm looking for Jackson." Yalana took another photograph out of her pocket.

"You saw the doctor?"

"If that's what you call the man on the hill, yes."

The woman shivered. "It was a bad trade."

"What did the man on the hill do to you?" There was time enough to drag Jackson away from this pit stain of a place and shoot the man on the hill before dawn.

"Nothing. He did nothing." The thin woman shrugged. "But, your man." She touched the photograph. "He's dying. He's lying there, sweating, dying. Sick. He's sick. No one can make him better."

Yalana didn't try to hide her relief. "He's breathing. That's all that matters. Show me where he is. I'll pay you. Food rations. Medicine. Whatever you want."

The woman rubbed at her arm.

"Clothes?" Yalana guessed. "I have more."

"Bottled water?" The woman's eyes were wide with hope.

"I'll give you a case if you show me where Jackson is and walk us to the docks."

Eagerly the woman sprinted ahead into the crowds.

Yalana followed, not quite running—because these weren't the kind of people who took well to sudden changes—but keeping pace and following to a rickety shack under a huddle of blackened palm trees. There was a ladder of sorts rather than stairs. She took the rungs two at a time and pushed away the blanket hanging between the walls, the only protection from the snow outside.

The air smelled sour. Rotting flesh and fermenting fluids had never been so welcome.

"Jackson?"

There was a wheezing breath from a dark corner.

Yalana held up the orb.

Jackson lay on the floor, clothes ripped and skin bloody from scratching. His eyes were half-open and he was too dehydrated to sweat.

"You're alive." She smiled.

"He's dying," the other woman said.

"He's been dying for weeks." Yalana looked around for a way to carry Jackson. "Everyone else died within seventy-two hours of contracting the virus. But Jackson is alive. And there's no one else sick on Junkyard. Do you know what that means?"

The woman shook her head.

"It means he found a vaccine of some kind. A way to slow the virus." But there was nothing to carry him with.

Yalana tore the blanket away and rushed back to the party outside.

The purple-haired man stood there, casually talking with someone. Watching her with sharp eyes.

She ignored him. "I need four or five strong people to carry a man for me."

Someone in the crowd snickered.

"Free passage to the mainland for anyone who helps me. No border check. No questions asked."

"You think your boat's still there?" a woman's voice scoffed.

Yalana smiled. "My boat is waiting and there's a coast guard cutter standing guard. I need a man carried. Now. free passage to the mainland. This might be the last offer anyone makes in a while." She turned and marched back to the hut.

The sound of several people hurrying along behind her made it clear that someone had listened. There were five in all. Two women who looked older than they probably were. Three men who looked barely out of their teens, if they were at all.

"This man is sick but not contagious," Yalana said. "Lift him, carry him to my boat, and you can all come with me. Or you can take the supplies I brought in case I needed to stay. Water. Clothes. Medicine. Addiction treatments. Radios. I have everything you could need."

She stepped back and let them reach for Jackson. He moaned in distress, and it was the most beautiful sound she'd heard in weeks.

Their odd party cut through the edge of the Junkyard, following the curve of the land down to the port.

As the stranger at the party had predicted, there were people waiting, trying to access her boat. The ripple field was keeping them back for now. It wasn't a strong electric current, but strong enough to shock them and none of them were inebriated enough to walk through the moment of pain to reach the boat.

Yalana went in front of her people carrying Jackson. If the thieves needed somewhere to focus, then she'd be the one in the spotlight. She whistled, sharply, the sound cutting through the background noise. "Hello."

"Hello." The largest one had a heavy coat that had maybe, once upon a time, been blue or gray. Now it was a indistinct shadow of a color, but it was protection against the snow. "You're a pretty little fish, aren't you?"

"What do you want?" Yalana asked.

The lead man looked her up and down. Under the yellow dock light his skin was yellow. Swollen. With sores on his face. This specimen wasn't nearly as clean as the shark she'd tangled with earlier. "I want everything, pretty girl. Give that to me, and I let you live."

"No trade. Move aside."

The man stepped closer. "The trade is good. I like a—"

Yalana squeezed the trigger. There was a small hole in her coat pocket, not big, and not ideal for targeting, but she'd practiced with it for years. Rarely had a need to use this gun with actual bullets, but the shot went straight.

The man fell dead on the dock.

"No trade," Yalana repeated. "Anyone else have an offer?"

The mob who'd come with Yellow stared at her. One of them moved fast, grabbed her arm.

"Remove your hand," Yalana ordered.

He leered at her.

Yalana brushed her thumb across the heavy ring on her free hand, felt the slight click as it transformed from a large, domed gem to a much spikier weapon, and punched.

She cut into the men's neck and dragged her hand down. The wounds weren't deep, but they'd burn.

The would-be boat thief lost his grip and stumbled to his knees.

A boot to the face and he toppled into the filth-choked water of the port.

"No trade," she repeated.

The remaining thieves scattered.

Clicking her ring back in place, Yalana glanced over her shoulder. Her pack of new followers had been joined by the Shark Man. She raised an eyebrow at him. "Problems?"

"Angry little kitty cat."

"Kittens have claws. People should remember that." A wave of her hand and the ripple field fell. "All aboard, who's going. And a case of water for the thin woman."

The Shark Man stepped closer, almost crowding Yalana, but giving her enough room to sidestep if she wanted.

She didn't. "You had your trade. I told you I'd pay anything. Give you anything."

His eyes caressed her face like he was trying to burn the memory of her into his mind. "I made the right trade. But you... Won't you regret giving up the lover you're willing to kill for?"

"No." Unequivocally and without question.

Lightning flittered overhead, jumping between the clouds in the ever-present maelstrom.

In the storm's light, it almost seemed like the man's eyes glowed. "You will be back."

"Perhaps. But not for you."

"No?" He smiled as if he'd heard a joke. "You left your heart dancing in the moonlight. It's here now."

24

"Good for my heart. I've never used it before and I'll never need it in the future. Enjoy using it for whatever you think that kiss magically gave you. Everyone deserves to have dreams of moonlight without snow."

The man frowned. "Do you believe you're heartless already?"

"Check my pulse." She grabbed his hand and pulled two fingers to her neck. "Feel anything?" She waited as her boarding party loaded Jackson onto the boat. "Anything? No. There's nothing there." She dropped the man's hand. "I was born heartless."

"There's more to a heart than the beat of blood. There's love."

"Never had that either." Yalana stepped aboard the boat and pulled the rope loose from the mooring. "Any other cryptic messages for me before I leave?"

The man looked at the party of refugees hurrying to hide from the snow as the wind picked up. "Take care of them."

"I will."

"I'll see you when you get home."

"Not unless you have a much better boat than I do."

"Home is where the heart is."

She laughed. "Then I'll see you at home, in the darkness."

Let him keep her heart. She had what she needed now to create the vaccine, and her search was at an end.

SEVENTY

ON THE VIEW SCREEN, THE SOL SYSTEM DANCED. Planets glowed like phosphorescent pearls in the sea of space. Doctor Jeff Koenig, lead scientist on the Dauphin settlement project, traced the image of Earth with his finger. He'd been born on Earth and left for the Delious system as soon as he could afford the emigration fees. Brilliant Delious, whose fourteen planets and all their many moons had been blasted into rubble by Hurluk world-destroyers. Only Delious Four remained, orbiting in isolation without her three moons.

He'd never meant to come back to Earth. Now he was leaving for a second time.

Earth had been too crowded when he'd left with his wife to start a new life out in the northern solar rim. Now the world-cities overflowed with refugees scattered by the Hurluk attacks. Accelerated terraforming on Dauphin wasn't the only plan to alleviate some of the housing pressure, but it was the only one that would show results within the next solar year.

Jeff frowned at the projection of Earth. How many of Sol's citizens really intended to emigrate to Dauphin?

Most people just wanted a place to abandon the refugees. But some would earn the money to buy their way free of the Sol system, and how many of those would come?

"Doctor Koenig?" Captain Mac of the *Terrance Lee* interrupted his reverie. "I need your crew to buckle down. We're hitting jump in twenty minutes."

"I thought everyone was settled." Jeff looked past the captain to the commons room where scientists mingled with the hired hands, all displaced workers paying back the cost of evacuation to the government. "Lawson."

"She's in the cargo bay."

Swearing, Jeff stalked down the hall. What had the congressional council been thinking when they assigned her to the team? But he knew the rumors; Doctor Bella Lawson threatened the wrong people, stepped on the wrong toes. So they'd dumped her on the Dauphin team.

If only he could dump her back.

She stood in an empty shuttle slot, staring at the bay door.

"Doctor Lawson?" Jeff said.

She pivoted, slowly.

"We need to strap down for jump."

Lawson pinned him with an angry glare, jaw clenched. "I'll be in my cabin."

He didn't bother arguing. All he needed to do was survive her tantrums for three months. Once Dauphin was open for settlement he'd move on, and she'd be back at Sol University driving someone else crazy with her conspiracy theories.

Captain Mac slapped Jeff's shoulder. "Mighty fine planet. I'm amazed what t-formers can do nowadays."

Both hands full of boxes, Jeff settled for a grimace and a nod. Dauphin was amazing: rolling green hills, majestic blue mountains, space enough for all of the refugees from Delious, Escibul, and the rest of the northern solar rim. "They've done a lot in thirteen months."

Mac cleared his throat. "I'm off. The first colonists are entering quarantine on Europa today. Seventy days, round trip. Will Dauphin be ready when we arrive?"

"The terraforming is finished, all my team needs to do is clear land for the living spires to drop, and make sure the crop rotations are started and ready to feed everyone." He could already see the green fields filling with the towering metal spikes embedded in black dirt. The self-contained towers would house homes and businesses—and act as temporary orbitals if the Hurluk turned Dauphin to dust under their feet.

"Living spires have hydroponics," Captain Mac said.

"Ground-grown foods are better for the body. Better for the spire's environmental system too. You can only push hydroponics so far."

"Doctor Koenig!" Shon Orto, Jeff's second-in-command and the coordinator for the first wave of science teams, shook papers over his head as he charged up the landing plateau.

Captain Mac shook his head. "Humans already? I don't understand why we risk personnel on a planet that's still terraforming. We have robots for a reason."

"Robots need maintenance. One circuit blows and all of a sudden your terraforming robot is thinking: 'I say, this planet would look so much more scenic with some volcanoes all over the place'." Jeff shuddered. He looked at Shon. "How are things?"

"Interesting. I just got some new readings in."

"Right." Jeff handed Shon a box of basic vaccines and smiled at Captain Mac. "No rest for the weary."

"See you in a few months." The captain waved and walked back to his shuttle.

Shon shoved papers at Jeff. "We're having some trouble with the third continent's major fault line."

Jeff sighed. "That's just the kind of news I don't want to hear."

-------∿∿∿∿∿-------

By nightfall, when Jeff stumbled to his makeshift room in the main building, the *Terrance Lee* was a green blip entering the wormhole for her return to the Sol System.

He was stranded a galaxy away from home with five hundred strangers on an unstable planet.

Seventy days. He was only stranded for seventy days, then things would be well once again.

DAY 2 OF 70

"You idiot!" Bella Lawson raged at Shon Orto, spinning her chair away from the computer screen. "You should have loaded everyone back on the *Terrance Lee* the moment we touched down."

Jeff shook his head. "Doctor Lawson, I don't think—"

"I'm not surprised," she snarled at him. Lawson turned back to Shon. "The SOP for earthquakes on a t-forming planet is to evacuate until stabilization is confirmed."

"Time is not a luxury we have," Shon said. "We have contracts. We have to—"

"You won't do anything if you're dead." Lawson slammed down the readouts. "I can't believe anyone signed off on this planet. I told Congress we couldn't move forward with the SHORTMIN t-forming. It isn't safe. But a well-placed bribe speaks louder than facts."

The last thing Jeff wanted was to give Lawson a chance to rave about a corrupt Congress endangering colonization. He cleared his throat. "Sol System can't absorb more refugees. The ones from Delious have no choice, they don't have planets left to live on. But with the natives from Escibul pouring in as well, humanity needs room to expand. If people weren't convinced that the Hurluk are headed for them next, it wouldn't be so bad."

Lawson rolled her eyes. "There's no evidence to suggest the Hurluk will move to Echo Territory next. They can't use our wormhole technology. From the Delios System they have dozens of star systems to invade. If you want to suggest they'll move their planet-destroyers in a straight line you might as well evacuate the Sol System too. They're next in line after Escibul."

She took a deep breath and looked at the printouts again, then shook her head. "We need to evacuate. The data doesn't lie."

"We can't." Jeff held up a placating hand. "I agree, it's the standard operating procedure. But where are we going to go? There's no other habitable planet in system. We have no orbiting base. And we can't live in shuttles for the next three months."

Shon raised his hand. "Maybe you're overreacting? Dauphin was signed off on. The original t-form expert considered the planet stable. What are the other possibilities?"

With a frustrated sigh, Lawson looked back at the seismograph.

"Could this be part of the natural settling process?" Jeff prompted.

"Possibly." Lawson pursed her lips. "If Doctor Orto"—she cut a glare at Shon—"hadn't been drilling, it's possible the tremors would have gone unnoticed. I can't guarantee anything though."

"We're not asking you to." Shon threw his hands up in the air. "Look, just tell me how to fix it."

"Fix it?" She laughed. "You can't 'fix' a shaking planet, Doctor Orto. There's nothing to fix. This is part of the process. If you like, I can tell you exactly what's happening and why. Or what will happen next. But I can't undo this."

"Then what good are you?"

"Shon?" Angeliessa Sahn, the horticulturist, walked in smiling. Her expression froze when she saw Bella's hard glare. "I—I just needed to talk to Doctor Orto."

"We're having a private conference," Lawson said coldly.

"Shon, there's nothing more you can do here. Go see what Miss Sahn needs." Jeff watched Shon chase eagerly after the pretty blonde. Well, best of luck to him.

Jeff turned back to the t-form expert. "Give me facts. What are we dealing with?"

"SHORTMIN cuts the standard terraforming time from six years plus colonization to ten months by cutting out two of the three ice age stages. All the glacial carving and continent sorting is done in six weeks."

"I know that. Tell me what this means." He stabbed the readout.

"I think it means we're entering third stage t-forming. Another ice age. This could be sixth stage settling, but I doubt it. Either way, we won't know until something drastic happens, or doesn't. SHORTMIN was never tested on a large planet. Dauphin is the lab rat. We shouldn't be here."

He was getting tired of the repetition. "We don't have a choice." Jeff stared at the readouts as though wishing would change them. He sighed. "I hope you're wrong."

"Dr. Koenig," she said, "if I was wrong on a regular basis, they'd have had no need to ship me off-world."

DAY 19 OF 70

"I get germination in four hours and maturation in a week. Each plant produces enough for six people for the three weeks it fruits. I'm trying to push the next generation to fruiting in five days with a four week growing season—"

Lawson walked into the greenhouse, knocking aside a row of pots in her hurry. "Doctor Koenig, I need to speak to you."

"This is a private conference!" Angeliessa snapped, moving to right the pots.

Jeff sighed, aware that he was caught in the crossfire of the first civil war on Dauphin. "Can it wait thirty minutes?"

"No."

"Fine." He smiled at Angeliessa. "Excuse me, I'll be right back." Jeff followed Lawson out of the greenhouse and across the lawn towards the gray, rectangular monstrosity that was both HQ and housing. "What's going on?"

She shoved a piece of paper at him.

Jeff frowned at the jumping line on the paper. "Read-outs from the drill probes? I thought you said it was something important."

"This is new. It's the readings from a seismograph on continent five."

"It's gibberish to me." He handed the read-out back.

She pointed to a spike that touched the top of the chart. "That's a major upheaval event."

"Are you sure?"

She gave him a withering look. "No. Maybe it was a butterfly jumping on the sensor? Of course I'm sure!"

"What do you want me to do?"

"Authorize a survey team to go to the fifth continent to check for visual confirmation, and assess damage."

Jeff watched Doctor Lawson's shuttle appear over the horizon, a black speck against the waning afternoon light, then refocused on what Shon was saying. "I'm sorry, repeat that, how much land is cleared?"

"Enough for the first four hundred spires. Bare minimum, that's four thousand people."

"We won't see spires with less than two thousand colonists," Jeff said. "Not with the news outlets running images of the Hurluk attacks night and day."

"Right." Shon scribbled on his pad. "I don't think we need to worry about that. My only concern is the native flora. It's the t-weed—fast-growing, adaptable, annoying at this stage. We needed it to produce the oxygen during t-forming, but it's going to clog the oxygen intake vents on the spires. I recommend a controlled burn followed by reseeding with a slower growing plant."

"Fine. Do you have the next section selected for clearing?"

"The north plateau. I just need Doctor Lawson to sign off on it."

"I'll send her over once she reports in." Jeff scrubbed his hands through his hair. Today wasn't the worst day they'd had, but he certainly hoped Doctor Lawson bore good news.

--------～～～～～～--------

The shuttle blew up dark dust as it settled. There was a soft "whump" as the anti-grav turned off and the ship dropped the last centimeter to the ground.

Jeff waited.

The doors cycled open and the survey crew exited, carrying a battered seismograph. Lawson followed, red-eyed and shaking.

"We need to evacuate. Now."

"What?"

"It's all gone. Fifth continent's been swallowed by a volcano. There's nothing but ash and lava, it's the size of Olympus Mons on Mars. We can't stay."

"We can't go! Do you want to sit on a shuttle for the next two months?"

"Yes!" Her breath stuttered as she sucked in air. "SOP—"

"SOP be hanged! We'll die of carbon monoxide poisoning on the shuttles. They aren't meant for long-term use. This continent is stable? Isn't it?"

She bit her lip. "Temporarily. This is Third Stage t-forming. Our weather patterns—"

"Will change. We might get cold. But it won't kill us in the next sixty days," Jeff said firmly.

"We have to adjust the genetics of the crops. The ash is going to cause a volcanic winter." She looked at him, eyes cold as the winter she was predicting. "Doctor Koenig, if things get worse, if the tremors hit us here, we *need* to evacuate."

Jeff shook his head. "We'll weather this, Bella. We have do."

Somehow. Somehow they would find a way.

Glass shattered. His bed jumped, screeching as it shimmied across the floor. Jeff rolled, landing hard on his knees, and scrambled to the shelter of his doorway. "Lawson?"

Something fell in her office, but no one answered.

"Shon?" Jeff pushed himself to his feet. He shook as he opened the blackout curtain. Pale pink moonlight streamed in on the wreckage of his study. Grabbing a flashlight, he checked Lawson's office first. She wasn't there.

How much would Congress fine him for losing a t-form specialist?

Aftershocks rocked the ground. Jeff stumbled, throwing an arm out for balance. "Lawson? Shon? Where are you?"

Fire backlit the skeleton of the wooden barn. A soot-covered Shon ran up to meet him. "What is this?" Shon said. "I was checking the barn before I went to bed and..." He waved his hand at the chaos.

The barn was burning—Jeff made a mental note to find out who hadn't secured the flammables in the appropriate locker—part of the shuttle bay roof had collapsed, and the greenhouse had been reduced to slivers of glass.

"Why didn't we get a warning?" Shon looked around in confusion. "Where is Angeliessa?"

Jeff glared at him as the ground shuddered. "How should I know? Where is Lawson? She's the one responsible for tracking these things."

Shon pointed across to the shuttle bays. "Shouting at someone."

"Go round up the science staff, we're meeting in ten minutes."

--------～∧∨∧∧∧--------

Jeff pushed tables aside to make space for the meeting in the cafeteria. Outside, workers shouted as they tried to corral the animals and put out the fire.

"Is this the meeting place?" A short, balding man with a wiry build shuffled into the room, laden with paperwork.

Jeff didn't recognize him. He set the last chair in place and frowned. "I'm Doctor Koenig, the project director. Who are you?"

"Doctor Berrans." The little man didn't offer a hand. He dropped his papers on the table and smirked. "I'm actually here with the EPP."

The broad smile only made Jeff want to punch him. "The what?"

"Energy Planet Program. Orator Rens pushed it through Congress a few months ago. Very important. Cutting edge. Turn the entire inner planet, the unnamed rock spiralling into the sun, into an energy source."

His fists clenched. "Isn't that a considerable waste of resources? We'll lose everything we put there when the planet falls into the sun."

"That won't happen for centuries," Berrans said. "Considering all the information we'll gain from our science stations the waste is negligible."

"Never mind." Jeff shook his head. "Why didn't you introduce yourself when I arrived?"

"Why would I have?" Doctor Berrans asked in surprise. "I'm the senior project director. Not that I would comment on your lack of introduction, I realize most of the personnel are working on your project. But since I arrived first—"

"You weren't supposed to be here at all! The EPP was scheduled to start with the fourth wave of colonists."

Doctor Berrans waved his hand. "The sooner I start, the sooner we have the energy sump."

"Right now we need a way to get off Dauphin and survive until Captain Mac comes back." Jeff looked at the rest of the frowning science staff: Shon, Angeliessa, Lawson… "Where's the shuttle rep, and Doctor Keeler?"

"Keeler is corralling the animals with his workers," Shon said. "He told me to tell you he doesn't care what happens as long as we promise not to destroy anything else. Marcus is still at the shuttle bay assessing damage."

"We'll start without them." Jeff turned to glare at Lawson. "Why weren't we warned this was coming?"

"Because we have no sensor grid system or seismograph in our area," she said with cold calm.

Jeff swore.

"What's happening to Dauphin?" Angeliessa asked. "I put out the cold-tolerant crops like Doctor Lawson ordered. But I don't have crops engineered to handle earthquakes."

"Dauphin is entering Third Stage terra-forming," Lawson said.

"Which is what?" Angeliessa asked.

"Earthquakes, upheaval events, drastic changes in topography, and it ends with a cataclysmic ice age." Lawson folded her arms across her chest.

An ELE, an extinction-level event. The thought made Jeff's blood run cold. "This isn't Third Stage. SHORTMIN

39

drops the t-forming process from five stages to three, and the ELE you're describing has already happened on Dauphin. This is something else."

"The tests for SHORTMIN were performed on asteroids and moons much smaller than Dauphin. I don't think the forced thaw of the ice age that ends the Third Stage was enough to lock the tectonic plates." Lawson paused, then set her lips in a thin line. "We need to evacuate."

"Maybe things will settle down," Angeliessa protested. "Normal planets have 'quakes, don't they?"

Lawson glanced at Jeff. "I've been tracking the tremors on the other continents. They're increasing in frequency and intensity. The new volcano on the fifth continent is primed to erupt again. We're already seeing the ash in the air. It's only going to get worse."

"Where do we go?" Shon asked. "What was the plan for this?"

"We move to the orbital support," Doctor Berrans said. The grating smile reappeared. "SOP."

Jeff glared at the obnoxious man. "We don't have orbital support. The Congressional Space Fleet is helping with evacuation of Escibul. The orators didn't think a ship could be spared for orbital support when the planet was stable and habitable."

"Idiots," Lawson hissed.

"That's not lawful!" Berrans sputtered. "I must file a complaint. Orator Rens will hear about this."

"What do we do?" Shon asked, reaching for Angeliessa's hand.

"We evacuate on the shuttles and hope we can hold off until the *Terrance Lee* arrives in system. Maybe do a slow burn towards the wormhole," Jeff said. "What else could we do?"

Doctor Berrans raised his hand.

Jeff gave him a cold look. "Yes?"

"On the spiral planet we have a research station. Nineteen burrowing drones to act as housing and room for hydroponics. The atmosphere is rich in oxygen. If Miss Sahn"—he nodded curtly at Angeliessa—"will work on hydroponics, we can stay there for several weeks."

"What happens after several weeks?" Shon asked.

Doctor Berrans sneered. "We run out of water, obviously. That close to the sun no water would stay in a liquid state for long."

"I vote for the shuttles," Lawson said.

"We'll suffocate," Berrans argued.

"We can adjust for respiration rates; we can't cut water rations."

"I need a few weeks to fix the shuttle's hydroponics and add algae tanks to purify the air," Angeliessa said.

"We don't have that kind of time." Lawson shook her head. "You'll have to do that in orbit."

Jeff stood. "We'll go to the spiral planet, regroup, outfit the shuttles, and leave for the wormhole. I want the first group evacuating in three days."

DAY 36 OF 70

The long-range scanner, meant to warn the colony if Hurluks came, sat silent in the corner. Jeff tapped his pen on the empty desktop, staring at the blank screen as if will alone could make the *Terrance Lee* appear. Thirty-four days, just keep them all safe for thirty-four days.

Shon Orto knocked on the door and let himself in. "We've got a problem."

Jeff sighed, rocking his chair back. "Another one?"

"We have nine shuttles, each with an optimal load of thirty people."

"Angeliessa's algae tanks will give us enough oxygen for the rest. We only have just over four hundred people on planet—"

Shon's face turned stoic. "Four hundred ninety-seven."

Jeff shook his head. "No we don't, we have—"

"Doctor Berrans' team wasn't part of the count."

"We only have nine shuttles." Jeff swore. "That was one less than I requisitioned. Didn't Berrans get any?"

"He signed for five," Shon said. "Which would have covered his team and their equipment—"

"But someone in Congress decided we didn't really need those shuttles," Jeff finished for him. "I want to think our shuttles are helping the evacuation effort, not ferrying some lobbyist around."

Shon grimaced. "We could dream. But it still doesn't give us the room. As it is, we have seven shuttles total. One is scrap, the other won't be space worthy without major repairs. Anyway I set this up, we can't take everyone. Someone has to stay."

"Not on Dauphin. We'll go to the spiral planet." Jeff made a mental note to name the place when they got there. "And then we'll sort it out. Maybe we can find a way to extend our survival time there."

Cold wind whipped ash into drifts along the edge of buildings, covering everything in a fine layer of grit. Another volcano had erupted while they slept, this one closer to the valley. It was only a matter of time before the little home they'd built was devoured by lava.

He went to the empty office, staring at the blank wall, wishing desperately for a drink to drown reality for a few hours.

"Jeff?" Lawson slipped in, shutting the door behind her. "The first shuttle is ready to go. Why aren't you on it?"

"I'm the project lead. I need to make sure everyone gets off safe."

"This shuttle is getting away. I'm not sure that next one will. Your family will want to see you again..."

She was supposed to be shipping out on that shuttle; she wanted to put him there instead. For the first time since the earthquakes started, he smiled. "My family's dead, Bella. They were on Delious Seven when it was destroyed. I was on Delious Four, attending a conference. If I'd taken them with me..."

Lawson hesitated, then a faint blush dusted her cheeks. "I met you there. When my ex-fiancé came to yell at me, you stepped in."

Jeff blinked. He vaguely recalled a thin, dark-haired woman, and a drunk. "It's been a long time. You two never got back together?"

"No. I wanted something he couldn't offer." Her smile

turned bitter. "It's ancient history. And you don't have time to talk."

"Send this instead." Jeff patted the long-range scanner. "Seeing Captain Mac arrive early will do more for morale than I can."

DAY 41 OF 70

The skulking gray hulk of Dauphin fell away. Beautiful, hope-filled, Dauphin. Dreams turned to dust.

Bella slipped her hand into his and squeezed. "I'm sorry."

"So am I."

DAY 59 OF 70

Kicks were the only language the power converter understood. Jeff started each day by communicating forcefully with the machine. To stop the cold air from turning his testicles to icicles while he slept, he had to kick the thing again in the evening.

"Jeff?" Shon Orto walked in wearing a sweat-soaked undershirt and regulation pants cut to the knees.

"It's working again."

"Good. Berrans is on the radio."

He twisted his neck, working out a crick. "About time we got those things up and running." Jeff took over the radio, the only way to communicate when daylight temperatures made leaving the buried buildings a death sentence. "Koenig here."

"I found a way to extend our water supply," Berrans said.

"How long?"

"Months. Dauphin was dry when it was t-formed. The water was brought in from ice rings around the third planet. We could fill a shuttle and bring it in. We could even use the broken shuttle as an ice mule, just tug it along behind. The ice won't need oxygen or gravity."

"Do we have the fuel for that?"

"As much as we could ever want. The shuttles use charged solar cells."

And sunlight was not something cloudless Spiral was lacking. "Contact the pilots. I'm dying for a real bath."

DAY 70 OF 70

Jeff ran a manual check on the long-range radar, pinging the distant probes, waiting for the reply. The probes responded. The endless night of space stayed empty.

"Shon?" Jeff walked into the living area. Quarters were cramped, for now, but they were surviving.

The younger man looked up from the table where he was playing a scratch game of checkers with his new wife. "Any news?"

"Can we get one of the shuttles to check their long-range?"

"Still no Captain Mac?"

"I'm seeing nothing."

"He might be delayed," Angeliessa said. "Maybe loading took longer than planned."

"Probably." Jeff forced a smile. He left the common room to hide in his own small apartment, not willing to voice his secret fear. The Hurluk only needed to go in a straight line from Escibul to Earth.

DAY 82 OF 70

"The only thing we can do is send a shuttle to the Sol System for a ship," someone argued over the radio. Jeff had lost track of the argument thirty minutes ago. They'd gone from constructive ideas to hysteria in record time.

Shon leaned over and hit the com button. "The stresses of re-entry into real space will rip the hull apart. You'll be shrapnel on the edge of inhabited space."

"Staying here is death!" another man screamed. "We have to leave before this planet hits the sun. How many years do we have before the heat broils us alive in these tombs?"

"Hundreds of years," Berrans said.

Jeff took the radio to stop the shouting match. "This isn't death. It just isn't a good life. This is sustainable, and until a larger vessel arrives to rescue us the only thing we can do is concentrate on sustaining life. Someone will find us before Spiral reaches a critical orbit."

He shut the radio off and covered his eyes before anyone could say, "Hurluk."

"Someone's going to try and take a shuttle," Shon said.

"There's no way to stop them," Jeff answered.

Sitting beside Shon, Angeliessa rubbed her growing belly. "If we reorganized the housing, that might make people less antsy. Everyone was tossed together at random. If we had more couples…"

Jeff nodded. It might be just enough to keep people sane. And trying it was better than doing nothing.

DAY 84 OF 70

Shuttle Four cruised across the radar screen, an insignificant green speck representing twenty-seven desperate lives.

Bella pushed the curtain to Jeff's living area aside. "Aren't you coming out? Dauphin is rising against the moons. It's almost pretty, from here."

"What does the surface look like?"

"Red and boiling." She tugged at his hand, a playful smile on her lips. "Come on. We all need fresh air. We only have an hour before the temperatures get too low. Watching the screen won't change anything."

He bit his lip. Bella leaned closer. Jeff gave in. "I'm coming."

DAY 648 ON SPIRAL

Prying the back panel off the long-range scanner, Jeff scrounged for wires to fix the cooling unit. He tore three short wires out and put the panel back before pushing the scanner into the corner. Space was at a premium, especially with a baby on the way.

He wrapped his knuckles one more time on the scanner, trying to remember the old terror of abandonment, the nightmares that gave him sleepless nights when they'd first arrived.

But it was gone now, joining Dauphin and Earth in the world of distant dreams. Myths. Bedtime stories for tired children.

He gave the converter a warning kick as he walked back to the kitchen. Dinner was almost ready.

LEVEL NINE

ANDREA STOOD AT THE EDGE OF THE CLEARING, studying the opposing force. She counted three hundred and seven killerbots loaded with every armament the engineers could think of. They stood there, a lethal wall of AI menace separating her from her goal.

The bushes behind her shook. Puzzled, she watched a man roll into view. Lasers seared the bush, setting it on fire. The man stood up and brushed the dirt away. He looked... wholesome.

Andrea tried to find another word. Crazy? He only had a small destabilizer, no armor, no vanguard of cohorts.

"Hello." He smiled.

Andrea smiled back. "All alone?"

"No one else could play today. You?"

"Flying solo," Andrea confirmed.

"Can't figure out how to get past?" the man asked.

"I can't figure out how to get past without cheating," she corrected. "This is only level seven, I've gone past a dozen times. But I always cheat."

"You can't cheat the game."

"You can," Andrea said. "You aren't supposed to, but you can."

"How?" He looked over the massed infantry of death in confusion.

She knew what he was thinking. The gate leading to level eight was plain to see. All you had to do was charge in, kill all of the killerbots in your way, and run through the level gate.

"If you're very fast..." he began.

"No. Just lazy. Watch." Andrea lifted a small stone; she weighed it in her hand. "Watch." She threw the rock, arcing it into the center of the killerbots.

As a unit, the droids turned and opened fire on each other. Within seconds there was nothing left of the wall of death but the hiss of cooling metal.

"Impossible. It must be a system glitch. They are programmed so they can't attack each other."

"They each attack the rock and most of them miss," Andrea said. "If the rock shatters it gets even better. Then they start shooting at the fragments."

"And they don't reset?" Intrigue and respect were written on the man's face.

"No," Andrea said. "It really is cheating though. I feel guilty just walking past their charred corpses."

"Is a melted droid really a corpse?" he asked.

Andrea punched a code into the controller at her wrist and the level reset.

The bushes shook again. This time an entire band of warriors rushed in, armed to the teeth and yelling.

"You need to go through?" one asked.

Andrea looked at the first stranger; he shook his head. "We just reset the level to try a different tactic. Not enough challenge the first time," she said.

"Mind if we charge through?" one of the heavily-armed men asked.

"Go for it."

Andrea and the wholesome man with the charming smile watched as the band of berserkers rushed the killerbots.

"We could try that," he suggested.

"They lost two people."

"Ah, good point. The odds aren't in our favor."

"Any suggestions?" Andrea asked as the level reset yet again.

The man picked up a rock.

They stepped through the level eight gate casually—almost too casually. Andrea had to grab the man by his shirt to keep him from making a fatal mistake.

"Trip wires under the leaves on the path," she explained.

"Ah," he looked down at the jungle path in front of them. "How do we avoid the trip wires?"

"See the wood planks outlining the path?"

He looked at the narrow span of wood. "Yes."

"Stay on that until we hit the clearing." Andrea balanced easily on the beam and waited for him to follow before she began moving. "The wires trigger the killerbots and skydroids on the other end. If you don't trigger the wires the 'bots don't come out."

"I thought the rules said you had to stay on the path," the man said.

"The rules were written by the same people who designed the killerbots. Think about it."

"Good point. I suppose they aren't rooting for the gamers."

"If they are, I've never noticed."

They moved through the artificial jungle, listening to the sounds ahead. A battle raged and fell suddenly silent.

"Do you think the berserkers died?"

"Charging doesn't work on this level. I've seen lots of groups try that and it never works. Level seven is the last one you can survive by charging. By eight, you need actual tactics."

"Do you play a lot?" the man asked politely.

Andrea looked at him, weighing her possible responses. "I play when I can, but it isn't often."

"Do you always come alone?"

"Do you?"

The man laughed. "I'm not trying to pry. I'm harmless. Really. And yes, I usually play alone."

"But you pick up the odd damsel in distress if you happen upon them?"

"Nope. Never met one. Although I don't mind picking up beautiful women who know how to cheat two levels in a row."

"Do you meet many?" Andrea asked.

"Nope. But after I met you, who else could I need?" His smile was dazzling.

Andrea snorted. "Nice line. But what you're going to want is someone who knows how to get past level nine, because I don't."

They stepped into an empty clearing with monumental buildings on each side. The doors to the buildings were closed, locking in the hordes of death.

The level gate loomed ahead of them.

"Suggestions?" the man asked.

"Level nine is dark, pitch black. Outside light sources don't work. The level gate is to the left but there's a cliff and a river between you and the gate. I've died in each of them. And there's a couple of killerbots. It never seems like a huge number but there are enough."

"Maybe we should try splitting up? One go left, the other go right?" he suggested.

"Bad plan. There are synergy bombs. If you and your buddy stand on the corresponding demolition plants at the same time, everyone in the level dies."

"Great." He checked his charge. "So, want to try again if we die?"

Andrea blinked at the thought. "I've got to get to work."

"Maybe we can meet up later? Where are you at?"

"Tetraterren, Alpha Side," Andrea said. "You?"

"Homely." A planet on the far side of the system.

"Thank goodness for faster-than-light relays, right?"

"Right."

"Our best bet is to try not to die," Andrea said. "Failing that, remember every detail you can so you can map the level when you die."

"When are you coming to play next?" the man asked.

Andrea shrugged. "I don't know." She stepped into the darkness of level nine.

Five minutes later, simulated leg broken, a killerbot honed in on Andrea. She shot out its sensors, trying to buy herself a few more seconds in the game.

Light flashed, a fire flare. "I'll find you!" the stranger shouted as he died.

The killerbots fired. Andrea died. The black and green grid of the ten-by-ten game room replaced the encircling dark of level nine. Andrea checked her watch. "Flippers!" Her shuttle for the space station took off in ten minutes.

She raced out the door, stripping her game suit as she went. She tossed the controls to the tech outside with a smile and grabbed her raincoat from the hangar.

"Good game?" the tech asked as she pushed herself out the door.

"The best!"

He'd find her—or she'd find him. And together, they'd figure out a way to conquer level nine.

RED PLANET REFUGEES

Blue lightning arched through red clouds boiling on the horizon. The sun hung low, a reminder of the day to come, a reminder of searing heat and the outpost's dwindling water supply. I pulled another shirt off of the line and risked a peek at the dark horizon.

Nothing.

The distant galaxies were too faint to be seen, and there were no near stars. We were the last outpost, the last human refuge before nothingness. But I didn't care about that; I was looking for the ice ship.

Every year it was a race. The original colonists were left with a single vessel to conduct basic observations and experiments. When the domes failed, that single ship moved my ancestors to the outpost monitoring the storm world. And now that one ship collected ice from the rings farther out to give us the water we needed to survive.

I didn't expect them today, or tomorrow, or even soon. We still had six months' worth of water left, if nothing went wrong. We could survive that.

But I still looked.

Taking the last shirt off the line, I waved to my neighbor. The gray-haired matron was the eldest of her small clan and the only one I knew on sight. The rest she kept cloistered inside their dome, safe from the radiation of the sun. I didn't have anyone protecting me. I didn't have anyone to protect. My only brother left after his wife and son died. My parents died years before that in a rationing scare; we'd survived while they wasted away from dehydration.

Instinctively, I checked the water levels as I walked inside. All the monitors showed the tank three-quarters full. Good enough for now.

I turned on the radio as I dumped clean linens on my make-shift bed and debated hanging my last few wet things on the line.

"Good morning everyone! This is Joe and Jo! Twenty-three minutes to full sunrise and it's already one hundred and ten outside. Looks like it'll be a hot one!" Joe yelled through the radio.

His wife, Jo, came on with a higher-pitched but equally-enthusiastic tone. "Hiya folks! Are you all ready for the day? Is your laundry in? Your dishes washed? Great! Because we have a full load of fun for you!"

I tossed my last suits into my basket and walked back outside. They were mostly dry and if I pulled them in within an hour, nothing would burn.

Coming back, I sealed the door behind me as the Hilda's Children's Chorus sang the wake-up song. The radio chimed and the family in charge of monitoring water gave their daily report.

Everything was fine, water levels were great, consumption was slightly up in the greenhouse because of the new seedlings being at 'that stage', but things were expected to level out in about seventeen days.

The radio chimed again and Jo cut in. "That was great kids! I'm glad to hear you so perky on this hot, hot day!"

"And thank you to the Dugroot clan for watching our water supplies. It's a grave responsibility," Joe said, giving the word 'grave' extra emphasis, "and for the last eight generations the Dugroots have proven they're willing to sacrifice to see the rising generation watered."

"Now that we've had the good news, let's try some bad news!" Jo enthused.

"Over to you, Jessa!" Joe said.

The radio chimed as I slid into my usual seat and pulled my microphone close. I smiled just like my brother taught me and started talking. "It's a wonderful morning over here at Far Out Skywatch and let me tell you, folks, there is nothing to see. Not a blessed blip on the radar screen. We are well and truly alone. But that's the bad news; let's try some more good news!"

"You have good news?" Jo cut in from the radio's main control panel.

"Believe it or not, Jo, I do!" I said, matching her enthusiasm. "Last dark we got a call from the ice ship. They're doing well and they sent their letters home." I pulled out my notepad and started reading. "Johnny sends May his love and says he hopes to be home in time for the baby. Trounce says 'hiya' to Ma and his brother. Matthew wants to let his clan know he's learning piloting and catching now, and making them proud. And young Egglebert, who's on his first tour, sends to say 'hiya' to all the folks at home, the view is great, and he's loving everything, and then the captain cut him off." I paused, imaging the clans gathered around the radio for our communal morning show laughing.

"The good Captain Tryer says to tell y'all that the ship's fuel is at eighty-seven percent and they're catching extra ice with the new nets that we rigged last season. Everything is in good working order; food supplies and morale are high. They expect to spend another twelve weeks catching and hope to bring home extra water this season.

"That's all I got, folks. This is Far Out Skywatch, if something happens I'll let you know!"

Jo and Joe took over as I switched off my radio. As I folded clothes and bathed, Jo and Joe prattled on, telling jokes, discussing books, and asking questions of the various clans.

As they started the 'Too Hot to Talk' song, I pulled on my shoes to get the last of the laundry off the line.

I laughed at the stale jokes. There were only seventeen families that had survived the past two-hundred-plus years of hardships; eventually we'd run out of things to say. But Jo and Joe kept morale high while we waited each season for crops to grow in our dimly-lit gardens and the ship to return with ice, all the while praying to some deity none of us knew that one day the nations that had sent our forefathers out would come back to rescue us.

I paused by the sealed door and touched the little calendar that my father had left.

Eighty-eight. Eighty-eight seasons until inbreeding, faulty technology, or lack of food killed us. The first refugees to arrive at the outpost had calculated how long they thought we could survive and made the calendar. By now most people had thrown theirs away in despair, but I kept ours, carefully removing one number each season, wondering if my ancestors who had carved the 324 pieces of wood ever imagined that we would still be on this planet when the wood ran out.

The radio chimed. I looked over my shoulder, frowning.

I really needed to get my laundry in before the temperatures soared, but it was rude to keep someone waiting.

The radio chimed again.

With a shrug I walked over to the radio station, my finger tracing down the line of lights to see who was trying to contact me.

Red four. Who was red four?

I hit the red light and my radar screen lit up green and black. I blinked as the radar blipped.

A blip?

What did that mean? My brother had taught me maintenance but he never mentioned blips.

I hustled to the back room where we kept the ancestors' books, diaries, and valuables tucked away for a future generation of refugees. I dragged my finger across the titles, trying to read fast enough to find the book I wanted in a hurry. There, written in Geek, a technician's manual for the radar array.

I pulled it down and scanned for a picture that matched my blipping radar. I found it a quarter of the way through the book. The caption read, 'Long Distance Array Radar Reading An Incoming Vessel.'

My heart stuttered as I skimmed the chapter. The black and green radar was the long-distance, deep-space radar, entirely different from the familiar red land-tracker that followed the ice ship landing.

I ran back to my radio and slammed my palm on the call button. "Hiya, folks, this is Far Out Skywatch and, um, according to the technician's manual I'm reading, the deep-space array has been activated by a, a..." I sucked in a long breath and spat out, "by an incoming hyperspace vessel that isn't broadcasting the pre-programmed security clearance.

"Folks." I grinned wildly. "We have visitors."

DREAM AWAY

"SIR, HOW WOULD YOU LIKE TO TAKE YOUR DREAM vacation today?"

The young woman smiling at Jazin as he tried to hurry down the packed commuter tunnel was a perky little thing. Cute button nose, cinnamon-colored hair, and pale-gold freckles on skin a few shades darker than her hair. She waved a synthpaper brochure at him. "Where do you want to go?"

"Home," Jazin said, avoiding eye contact. "My bank account doesn't match my dreams."

She stepped out from behind the table, her ivy-green skirt swirling as she moved. "I have dream vacations for all budgets."

"Yeah?" And he was going to get a promotion to a corner office. Just as soon as the moon turned blue. "Does this dream vacation come with paid leave?"

The young woman smiled impishly. "No leave time required. This really is a *dream* vacation." With a touch of her finger, the brochure projected a hologram of him on a white sand beach. "Do you know the average dream lasts less than five minutes? With Dream Away's new REMtech Dream 6K, you can have a week's worth of luxury in five minutes."

Jazin pushed the brochure away. "Thanks, but no thanks. I can't afford a vacation, real or otherwise."

"Oh, but you can!" she insisted. "Give me a minute, I'll give you the perfect day. Give me five minutes, and I'll give you a week in paradise. Give me an hour, and I can give you a lifetime!"

He shot her a skeptical glare. "You will give me a sticky chair to nap in that stinks of other people and hasn't been sanitized in a week. Thanks, but pass."

He sidestepped and kept walking.

"Come on," she cajoled, dancing to keep up. "Would it hurt to try it?"

"Yes. I'd like to pay my rent this week, thanks all the same."

She licked her lips and glanced back at the stall. "What if I... gave you a taste? For free."

He stopped outright and looked her over. "Sounds like you're pedaling hard addictives, lady."

"Oh, no!" She shook her head and her beaded earrings jingled a soft melody. "Dream Away's product is one hundred percent non-addictive."

Jazin rolled his eyes. "I bet. I nap, I walk away and the dream's forgotten in ten minutes anyway. Everybody knows dreams don't last."

"Dream Away dreams do." She placed a small, elegant hand on the crook of his arm and peered up at him, green eyes wide. "In one minute I can give you the perfect day. You want the corner office? It's yours. Want to be the star of your favorite sports team? Done. You want a day to catch up on your reading? I have all the books waiting for you. You'll feel the pages in your hands, smell the paper and ink, and when you open your eyes you'll remember the book just as if you'd spent the day reading."

He frowned. "And then I'll want another hit. Which will cost me—what—a day's wages? A week's? It's not worth it."

She shook her head determinedly. "Dream Away provides no more endorphins than you would get from a thirty minute run at the gym. And while we can't burn calories for you like a run will, we can offer you a reduction of mental stress. You won't get a real sunburn at the pool in the Jawamai Mountains. You won't really eat draris fruit in the orchards of the Old King. The new friends you meet won't be real. But you'll remember all of it like it was. It really is the perfect vacation."

"How will I remember it?" he demanded, gripping his briefcase tighter. "Are you going to dribble fruit juice on my chin?"

"Even things you experience while awake are merely secondary sensations processed by the brain. Originally created to combat depression, the REMtech Dream 6K is the delightful side outcome of Dr Wria's research into retraining brains after traumatic injury. While it initially relied on pre-programmed dreamscapes, the new Dream Away is now sensitive enough to respond to sensations perceived by your brain, allowing you to design your own dream as you experience it."

"So you can't guarantee I won't have a nightmare." He knew there had to be a catch. There was *always* a catch.

The girl hooked her arm through his elbow and steered him toward the store. Brightly-colored travel calendars and pictures of famous buildings lined the walls. "We do exert a little control," she said reassuringly. "The REM Tech Dream 6K enhances your dream thoughts by triggering the respective neurons. You think of a fruit and by your first dream-bite, you will taste the perfect fruit. Using the same technology, we can steer dreams so that you stay in a pleasant and happy state, whatever that may be for you." She shrugged. "Or not. We don't judge."

He watched as one of the booths opened and a smiling man walked out, chatting happily with a blue-skinned woman wearing the same green skirt as the girl. The man wore a low-level maintenance worker's uniform, but instead of a laborer's perpetual frown, he looked as if he'd never had a bad day.

"A regular customer," the girl said. "He comes in every few days for a three-minute dream. Says it's like getting an extra weekend."

"And how much of his pay are you stealing?"

"Small packages have small prices," she said. "He pays two credits, only a quarter hour's wages for him. Fifteen minutes' worth of pay and he gets three days in paradise."

Jazin snorted. "And I bet he can't tell reality from fairyland anymore."

Her smile grew amused. "Dream Away does complete product testing before putting anything on the market. You'll find, as our researchers did, that it is easy to differentiate dreams from reality. You retain the memory of the place, but the human mind always knows where it is. That gentleman has been doing classes and training prep during his dream sessions. Dream Away is helping him get a better job."

The blue-skinned girl started chatting up another prospective customer in the busy transit corridor.

He sighed. That was life, wasn't it? Rush to work, hustle all day, rush to catch the next tram home. Every day was regulated down to the minute. His pay meant he had sixty minutes a week of running water, four hours a week of electricity, and a single meal box with seventeen nutritional meals a week. The other meals he either had to skip or spend money on at a company restaurant.

The girl nudged his shoulder. "One minute and I'll make all your cares go away."

"One minute?"

"The perfect day. And the first time is free."

"Fine." Jazin waved to the back of the store. "Fine. I'll try it. It's the only way you'll let me go."

"You won't be disappointed!" she bubbled. Grabbing his hand, she dragged him back to a small parlor painted entirely black. "Don't worry about the color. This is just to keep light reflection down. Please, have a seat."

A black plethasynth chair sat in the middle of the room with a green light shining out of diodes along the headrest. "That's it?"

"The REMtech Dream 6K is a very advanced machine. We don't need wires and cables everywhere to do this. After all, this is the age of nanotech!"

"All right." Reluctantly he shrugged off his coat. "Um..."

The girl pointed to the wall. "There is a locker there. You can code it to your handprint just like the lockers at work."

The ubiquitous Quaslin LockerShop lockers. Seventy years ago Quaslin had been a minor repair company, and now a person couldn't turn around without seeing their logo plastered on some piece of metal. That was the advantages of having one of the only metal refineries left in operation. But at least he knew his belongings would be safe.

He tucked his briefcase and coat in, double checked the lock, and reset the code.

"You'll only be asleep for a minute," the girl soothed.

Spoken like a woman who wouldn't lose her job if the boss found out she'd been casual with a company briefcase. It didn't matter that he didn't have rank, or secrets to hide; the company was in open conflict with three other major corporations, and any sign of indiscretion meant a pink slip and your name on the station blacklist.

"Sit here, sir, and I'll adjust everything for your optimal comfort."

Jazin eyed the chair and then heaved a sigh. "Fine." He sat down and noticed wrist braces on the arms of the seat.

The girl followed his worried gaze. "Those are there for your safety. About twenty percent of our clients experience sleep-walking tendencies, involuntary and uncontrolled movement, while dreaming. The straps keep you from waking up with a black eye." She snapped the locks shut and a screen on the ceiling lit up.

The words I AM FULLY AWAKE glowed pink in the darkness.

"What's that?"

"That is the voice control panel for the restraints. When you wake up you read the words provided and the machine will release you. Would you like to try it?"

"I am fully awake," Jazin read aloud.

The word RHUBARB appeared in the same soft glow.

"Rhubarb," Jazin read obediently.

The restraints unsnapped with metallic click.

"Ready for your perfect day?" the girl asked as she locked him back in.

He settled back into the soft arms of the machine. "Sure, let's do this."

"Where would you like your perfect day to be?"

Jazin shook his head. "I don't know. The beach sounds nice. I've never been there."

"Then off to the beach it is. Sweet dreams!"

The lights dimmed and he heard the door shut. He took a deep breath, blinked, and he was standing on the beach with a hot sun beating down on his bare arms.

A white bird swooped overhead, shrieking. Just ahead, a shack of some kind looked like it was selling drinks. It seemed like a promising direction.

She lifted the ident card off the corpse in the chair. Jazin Reirs, software technician, second-class. Middle-aged, overweight, single, and stupid as a box of rocks. He'd carried encrypted documents to and from work every day and never known the value. Poor fool. If he had guessed, maybe he could have sold the papers and bought some protection.

Her ear comm crackled. "How is our friend?"

"Dreaming. Permanently. I have everything we need."

"Then get out. We have another target for you."

She folded the papers and tucked them into a locked carry-case hidden in the garter on her thigh, then locked the dream parlor behind her. The nice young lady she'd rented the room from waved as she showed another prospective client the latest in TuyongTech virtual reality.

Experience the beach in real time, sand in your shoes is extra!

It was true what they said: people who spent their lives dreaming of a better future never were awake enough to make one.

THE BOY NAMED NO

TWO STRAIGHT LINES OF UNWANTED WAIFS STOOD AT military attention by their cots. Matron L. R. Rus' heels clicked as she marched down the rows, inspecting hospital corners, checking under the beds for debris, ordering hands held out so she could verify they were properly scrubbed.

The last cot stood alone, blankets folded at the end of the bed where the orderly had placed them the night before. The cot's tow-headed owner was missing.

Again.

Matron Rus scowled. "Justice Saber Rus, get out here this instant!" Not expecting much, she checked under the bed. Nothing. A twinge of clan pride kept her from screaming. He was a Rus; even if he was unwanted, at least he was intelligent.

She eyed his footlocker, then, with practiced ease, overrode his lock code. Shredded uniforms and a shredded gray bag.

Frustration boiling over, she turned to the boy across the aisle. "Where is Justice?"

"He left last night, ma'am."

She scrolled through her mental list of names, trying to place the dark-haired child. Virtuous Shield Pantros. Age six, large for his age and clan. Probably not a full Pantros.

"Why, Mister Shield, did you not inform anyone when Justice left?"

"We were told not to make any noise, ma'am." His dark brown gaze slid upward, watching her.

"You didn't consider the consequences of allowing him to wander away?"

"I did, ma'am. But I can't break the rules, ma'am," he said with infuriating calm.

Matron Rus smiled. "Rebellion by obedience, how very charming. Unit!" she bellowed. "Move out to the cafeteria. You will be fed when Mister Saber joins you."

The children marched out.

With a sigh, Matron Rus collected the tattered gray duffel and dropped it in the carbon recycler. It was always the first thing he destroyed when he threw a tantrum.

She opened the hall closet, looking for a replacement.

"Matron Laura?" a voice interrupted.

"Yes?"

Terssa Camlin Fisher stepped around the corner. "Unit Five just arrived in the kitchen and the little Rondros Pantros girl told me they were waiting for Justice. Where is he?"

"A very good question, Miss Camlin. He's run off again."

Terssa sighed. "The poor dear. He was so upset when the claims list came in yesterday and he wasn't on it."

"He'll never be on the claims list. He's been here for six years and his name has never been listed."

"Little Erinna Sandol Rus was listed this year, and she's nearly nine."

"Erinna's mother brought her to the crèche. The enforcers found Justice wrapped in a bag in a trash can." She slammed the closet door. "Children found in trash cans are not later claimed by their ecstatic family. Now, where are the gray duffels?"

"W-We're out. I can put in an order for more."

Matron Rus grumbled and opened the closet again. "No matter. If the boy didn't shred his things every time he was upset, he wouldn't need a new bag." She pulled out a navy blue bag meant for the children two years younger than Justice. Each year group had their own color, a simple strategy to help the children find their things. Writing names on the inside was the other half of the strategy, and the major sticking point for the little Rus boy.

"I'm going to wait for Justice. Keep an eye on the other children. They'll have to sleep in the cafeteria tonight. I don't want one of his cohorts smuggling him food."

"Yes, Matron."

She returned to the room, lost in thought. *If I were a six-year-old boy, where would I hide?*

Fan-shaped leaves rapping the windowsill drew her attention. The Aral mountains rose in the distance. Thick copses of pine, snow in high summer, and bitter cold tarns. Yes. That would tempt a boy away as the frost cleared from the grass.

Matron Rus took a seat on the boy's spotless footlocker and waited.

Early morning light brightened to noon. Noon warmth faded into early evening. Cold wind rushed down from the mountain heights. As the supper bell rang, she saw one shadow moving amid the lengthening shadows of the trees.

Over the windowsill two white ears appeared. A furry white face with distinctive black stripes followed. Ice-blue eyes glared and whiskers twitched.

Matron Rus stood up and brushed imaginary dust off her skirt. "Well, Mister Saber. Have you finally decided to grace the house with your presence?" She heard his stomach growl.

The little white tiger cub slunk over the windowsill, green burrs clinging to him. Blood matted the fur on his left leg.

"Playing rough were we, Mister Saber?"

Justice sat down in front of her and deliberately licked his paw as if to say she had no control over him.

"Stand up, Mister Saber. I demand an accounting."

The pale blue eyes narrowed. The cub straightened, shoulders arching back. He sat tall and kept growing taller, stretching and flowing out of the white tiger's form and into that of a chubby-cheeked blond boy with dark tan skin and ice-blue eyes.

The burrs fell to the floor with a papery whisper.

"Give me your hand," the matron ordered.

He held out his left hand for inspection.

"Neatly done. Why didn't you shift the injury away before you came in?"

"Didn't wanna," the boy whispered, his voice rasping.

"Hmmmm. Turn." She inspected him head to toe as he pivoted. "No other signs of injury." Although his ribs were showing. "How many times a week are you shifting?"

He shrugged. "Lots."

"You need to eat more if you are changing forms on a regular basis, Justice. If you are shifting more than once or twice a week, I need to know."

Her heart bled for the pathetic little boy. Unwanted. Unheeded.

And, may the ancestors forgive her, so unlovable. Prickly as an urchin. There were days she suspected the boy didn't want to be loved.

He glared at the ground, nose scrunched and lips tightly pursed.

So much for nice.

"Mister Saber, I asked you a question. I expect an answer. How often are you shifting?"

"Lots!" he wailed. The cub's bottom lip jutted out in a pout.

"Daily?"

"What's that mean?"

"Do you shift every day?"

A nod.

"More than once a day?"

Another nod.

Matron Rus sighed. "I expect you're hungry."

No response.

"Mister Rus, are you hungry?"

He shook his head. "I ate something."

"What?"

"I dunno. It hopped."

She blinked. "A rabbit? You ate one of the school rabbits?"

"Not a rabbit!" Justice said, sounding insulted. "It was black, and kinda crunchy. And small."

"A locust?"

"Do they look like giant grasshoppers?"

"Yes."

He nodded. "It tasted funny."

"You need more than a bug for dinner. Get dressed and I'll take you down to eat."

The cub nodded eagerly, a smile dimpling his cheeks.

She held out his blue duffel. "Your new bag."

The smile vanished.

"Justice," Matron Rus warned. "Every child at the crèche has their own bag. With name in it."

"It's no' my name," he muttered.

"Your name is Justice Saber Rus. You will write it in the bag, and then you may eat dinner."

He took the bag between thumb and forefinger—and dropped it on the floor.

Turning, the cub went to his locker and pulled out his clothes. He dressed slowly, with a furrowed brow of concentration. He turned to her, jaw set in a defiant line. "My name is not Justice Saber Rus."

"Yes, it is."

"That is your name for me," he said. "It's not my real name. My real name is what my family calls me."

Matron Rus closed her eyes. Would telling him the truth crush him? "Justice, the crèche is your family. We raised you. We named you. We're here for you."

"But you aren't my real family," the cub persisted.

"We're as real a family as you'll ever know."

Pale blue eyes narrowed. Justice growled.

"You are not here because I enjoy these arguments, Mister Saber. No one in the crèche is holding you hostage. We welcomed you in your infancy and gave you a home."

"Because no one else wants me," he whispered.

She sighed and sat on the footlocker, holding out a placating hand. "Not everyone can keep a child. There are times—"

"When it's okay to wrap a baby in a bag and put them in the trash?"

He'd been listening.

"No, Justice, there is never a time when that is acceptable."

Justice nodded. "I was stolen. A bad man took me from my real family, and threw me away. When my real family finds me I'll have a mommy and a daddy. And sisters. And cousins."

As fanciful delusions went, it wasn't half bad. "No one stole you, Justice."

"Yes they did! My real family wants me! They have a real name for me!"

Matron Rus stood and pulled a pen from her pocket. "We're not arguing. You are here. This is your life. Until such a time as your family arrives to rescue you, your name is Justice Saber Rus. Write it in the bag, and you may eat."

"No." He crossed his arms.

She held the pen out, adamant. "Write. Or you will go hungry."

Justice stood in front of her, bag at his feet, and glared.

The sun set. Night crawled past.

Terssa Camlin Fisher snuck into the room to get someone's stuffed doll so the rest of the unit could sleep downstairs. Still the cub glared.

As dawn light filtered through the trees, fat tears rolled down the cub's cheeks. He grabbed the pen and sat.

Another hour passed with Justice staring at the bag.

"Write your name," Matron Rus ordered as the break-fast bell rang.

Shaking with rage, Justice opened the bag. She watched the tears fall as he scowled at the white tag. He sniffed. He opened the pen, leaned forward, and scribbled. Then, dropping it all, he stormed out of the room.

Matron Rus waited until she heard his feet running to breakfast before she bent down to inspect the bag. Only one word was inscribed on the tag:

NO

She folded the duffel and put it in Justice's footlocker. Forty years as a crèche matron had taught her patience—and that sometimes, a small bend could break a child. Justice could find his bag now. If he didn't shred it, then they were taking the first step toward healthy adulthood.

And, who knew? Maybe someday the boy named No would find his real family.

THE DOG IS DEAD

A PALE HALF-MOON HUNG ABOVE THE PINE TREES AS I walked in the noon sun, wishing instead that I could run. It mocked me with the promise of a life I couldn't have, shouldn't want. The wind whispered, stirring the flowers around my feet as they wilted. I was no good at gardening.

I wasn't good at much, actually. But it was no big deal. Maybe a few hundred years ago when humans had eked out a living by growing their own food it would have mattered, but in the modern world where schooling was a matter of tissue programming and roles were chosen for everyone by a government program decades before they were born, being useful wasn't necessary.

The entire purpose of *my* life was to exist. My parents had money, which was nice. It meant they could afford to own land here on Earth and buy me a modest education when I turned ten: three hours of reading, writing, and basic mathematics programmed straight into my cerebrum.

When I was fifteen, my parents bought me a secondary education, allowing me to discuss classic literature with everyone else in my social strata. We'd all been programmed with the same six lectures, so our conversations usually devolved into recitations, seeing who could remember them best.

At eighteen I was tested, found intelligent enough to receive a basic civilian file (programmed into my head in fifteen minutes), and shunted into Slot 37B-12D5: housewife.

If my parents had been poor, we would have been relocated to Prima, the main lunar base that hung like a golden star over the moon's surface.

If they'd been wealthier, I would have received a fuller education that prepared me for more than balancing a check book.

If I'd been more intelligent, I would have earned a place among the scientists who filled Stellar base on the far side of the moon, the ones who'd be first chosen for any new colonies in the stars beyond.

In the secret watches of the night, when I stepped away from my cold bed to gaze at the stars, that's what I wished for.

Something new. A glimmer of opportunity to be someone else. To remove the choking grip of societal norms and replace it with the heady sensation of not knowing what would happen next.

But here, in the noon light, under a half moon white as the clouds, I knew I would never have those things. I knew it as a child, and I would remain faithful to that truth until the day I turned ninety-seven and reported to the hospital to be humanely put down, sure in the knowledge that some young girl would arrive at my house the next morning to wear my clothes and walk my dog, because that is what Citizen 37B-12D5 does three times a day, rain or shine.

Of course, it wasn't a real dog, which would be cruel. It was a Canine Companion with FeelReal-Furr and a life-like bark. None of my schooling included information on dogs, so I had no words to describe it...

Him... Her... It.

That bothered me.

I wished I knew what words to say if I ever brought my pet up in conversation, but I didn't. I never would.

It was black. It came to my knee. It was programmed to need five kilometers of walking every day, which ensured I received the necessary exercise for my age and meta-bolism. With one last wistful glance at the moon, I checked the mail (nothing) and returned to the house.

As I did every day, I watered a bowl of dead petunias on the front step, swept the wooden floors, and checked that the computer had ordered dinner for us.

We were having pot roast. Everyone on the block was having pot roast. As far as I knew, everyone in my social strata was eating pot roast tonight. With slightly over-cooked carrots and a choice of water or apple juice to drink.

I didn't want pot roast. I didn't want to water petunias. I didn't want to wait for another hour until my lawfully wedded husband arrived home from his government job to eat dinner.

I went to the door, twisting the handle, even though I knew it was futile.

A melodic chime signaled the end of my momentary rebellion. "This door is locked for your security. Please state the reason you wish this door opened at this time."

"I want to go outside." My hand dropped to my side. I knew it was fruitless. It wasn't in the script. Citizen 37B-

12D5 never went outside in the afternoon.

"Did you forget to check the mail?" the computer asked.

"No."

"Would you like to watch some television?" Unbidden, the television in the corner turned on, showing a comedy about life in the corporate world. "Your friends and neighbours all enjoy this show. Why not join them in a light-hearted laugh as Randi and Co. try to make Mister Meeker forget his glasses?"

"I don't wish to watch television. I want to go outside."

"Perhaps you would like to call a friend?" the computer suggested.

"I would like to go outside."

"Why don't you log in to your social network and plan a picnic? Everyone loves picnics." A screen on the kitchen table shimmered to life and showed a running stream of the thoughts of my 'friends'. They were all very similar; we did all have the same twenty-thousand-word vocabulary after all.

"Thank you," I lied to the computer. "That sounds very engaging."

I sat down and watched as people typed the lines from the show as it played behind me in the living room. As Mister Meeker outsmarted Randi and Co. once again, a gray car drove up to our house. My husband exited it, checked his tie, locked the door, and counted forty-eight steps precisely.

The door unlocked for him and he stepped inside. "Hello, dear. You look well. Did you have a good walk with the dog?"

"Yes." The word was past my lips before I even considered another option. "Dinner is ready."

"Good. I had a busy day. I'm hungry."

I mouthed the words with him. In four years living together, our conversation never varied. Sometimes I wondered if he was as robotic as the canine companion now lying inactive by the fake fireplace. "What would you like to drink?"

"Water, please."

I stood, and again rebellion flared. I arranged our dinner plates and gave us both apple juice. Instead of taking the eight carrots allotted to me, I piled all sixteen carrots on his plate and took both slices of meat. "Dinner is ready."

My husband took off his tie and looked at our plates. "D... d... d..."

"Your line is, 'Dinner looks delicious.'" I folded my napkin on my lap and waited for him to sit.

After a moment he sat beside me. "Dinner looks different."

"I tried something new today. You will like it."

I hoped I was lying. I hoped he hated it. I hoped he threw his plate and broke a window so I could run out through the glass and watch the moon set in the darkness.

He ate his carrots. "Dinner was delicious. Thank you."

And it was over.

Now he would go to shower, change into a bathrobe, and watch two hours and thirty-one minutes of television before yawning once and going to bed.

I sat at the table staring at the two slices of meat on my plate.

I was only hurting myself by not eating. No one else would notice. No one else would care. And if by some small chance I was able to resist food for days on end until I made myself sick, I would only be transferred to the hospital and be reprogrammed. Or put down.

I dumped the meat on the canine companion's food bowl, on top of the fake kibble I put in for verisimilitude. The canine companion could only eat on command and I'd never ordered it to eat before. Now I did. "Dog. Eat."

Wagging its tail, the robotic construct chewed on the real meat—and choked. Its eyes sizzled for a moment, flashing red, and then it fell over with a hollow clang.

My husband laughed at something on the television.

I walked over, standing in front of the screen so I could block his view.

"The dog is dead."

My husband struggled. This wasn't part of the script. This is not what we did every day. This was new.

I nearly clapped with joy. This was new! I didn't know his answer! I didn't know what came next!

"Why is the dog dead?"

"The dog ate food. The dog choked. The dog is dead."

My husband stood up and turned to look at the canine companion. "Dogs should not eat people food." He sat back down and laughed even though the television was showing a commercial for toothpaste.

Everyone loved that commercial. When I ordered groceries online on Tuesdays, the screen always told me it was the one my friends liked.

I wondered about that. Was there any other kind of toothpaste?

If I wanted to buy something that none of my friends had tried, would the computer let me? Would I like it if I did?

There was no way of knowing. I sat beside the dead dog. My husband watched his television shows and went to bed. The lights in the house turned off. The steady hum of electronics died as the computer decided we were asleep.

Why it followed his schedule and not mine, I wasn't sure. The computer would remind my husband to go to bed, but never me. Once he was home and I was safely locked inside, nothing else seemed to matter. Proof that the computer was just as dumb as everyone else.

I watched the moon set, Prima shining like a gem.

Was there someone out there who wanted to be me? Did that person have a number like I did, a place in society like mine? Or did they have a name?

I showered after the moon set, got dressed, and lay in bed waiting for sleep to come. It never did. I wasn't tired. I was bored. I wanted...

Something. I wanted to go outside.

When my husband woke up early, I picked up the dog and followed him to the door. This wasn't in the script. Fear filled his eyes.

"I'm putting the dog outside."

"I think the dog wants a walk." When in doubt, stick to the script.

We both looked at the spot where the canine companion should have been jumping with its tongue hanging out.

"Yes. I guess I should walk the dog."

He nodded. "Have a good day."

As the door closed, I shoved the dog's body in the way. The lock clicked shut and the television turned on the morning news.

I stepped outside as the reporter detailed what a beautiful morning drive it was today.

Canine companions couldn't walk on grass, so we always followed the sidewalk on a loop through the neighborhood, screened by pine trees. On the way I'd see glimpses of the highway in the distance. At one point, you could even see the spires of the city buildings. I didn't know which city; geography cost extra.

This morning I walked on the grass, watching it bend under my heavy tread. Each step smothered to death countless plant cells.

I was incautious.

Uncaring.

I reveled in their tragic demise.

I twisted the toe of my shoe into the turf, relishing the feel of grass dying under foot. I imagined little screams of plant terror echoing to the cold stars above. I imagined the gasp of shock and denial as someone from Prima looked down and saw me savagely destroying a plant they could never touch because they were banished from the very planet of their birth.

The sweet scent of cut grass invigorated me. I ran.

Over the lawns and past the pines I ran, to the edge of the highway where auto-piloted cars flew past, their passage whipping my hair up. My heart raced as I realized I could end it all here. None of those cars could stop. None of the drivers even knew how to.

I could leap and after a moment of blinding pain, everything would be over.

I jumped.

The cars stopped.

They hung in the air like frozen hummingbirds, unreal.

Tentatively, I reached out a hand to touch a bright red cruiser. The car was hot. The driver inside looked back at me, confused, uncertain. We were off script. Off the script. Off the page. Off the writing desk and floundering.

I stepped through the space between cars. Skipping, dancing. They moved around, resumed their flow. Everything was as it should be except that here and there—wherever I stepped—they froze. I was the queen of chaos, suspending the birds in their flight.

Life happened around me as I wandered down the lines of the highway. People went to work.

One car I stopped had an old man with a dark face, somber and sad. I knew without a word that he was on his way to the hospital to die. I stepped away and his car moved on, rolling with the tide of humanity to its destination, inevitable, unavoidable.

Inescapable.

I followed. It was that or find my way back to the pine trees and the quiet suburban house where my canine companion lay dead.

If I went back, the doors would lock.

If the doors locked, I'd never escape again.

If I never ran, I'd never know how far I could go.

THE LIES WE KNOW

"REMEMBER, YOU'RE ALL GOING TO DIE EVENTUALLY. Might as well make it worthwhile."

As pep talks went, the commander's was down with the likes of 'Let's all get killed!', but he seemed convinced he had a point. The problem was, he didn't. I knew he was wrong. My whole life had proved him wrong.

Most people died eventually. But life is all about probability and statistics. There are no absolutes. Even death, a penultimate absolute that claims 99.999999% of the population, isn't truly an absolute. There's always that .000001%. Me.

Everyone clamped their helmets tight shut against the vacuum of space. We were going into battle against overwhelming odds and we needed to make them underwhelming odds before the Kanfir ships reached the jump for the Euon Ri system.

Thirty-seven hours later, I was the only survivor, and the captured Kanfir flag ship was arguing with me.

"I cannot obey that order."

"Kendla sentient ship! I don't care what you think you can or cannot do, change course before we hit the sun!"

"I cannot obey that order. A senior line officer must enter the course change into the log book."

I banged my head on the soft, somewhat gummy edge of the ship's interface. "Is there a senior line officer left alive?"

"No."

Didn't think so. The Kanfir hadn't anticipated us swarming their ships with soldiers in aerial jets meant for orbital station work. The barges had closed, we'd shot off across the vacuum, and watched as the empty barges burn behind us. It was a suicide mission. Sort of. Not for me, per se, but for everyone else. "Are there any junior officers left alive?"

I didn't want to go into the sun, but this ship was the last one left with working navigation controls.

Sort of. The Kanfir captain had burned the override interface before we took their control room, but the ship itself was alive. I didn't know enough about the Kanfir to know if the ship was a species they'd caught and enslaved, or if they'd created these behemoths in some lab, but whatever the creature's history, it was bent on driving me to insanity.

"I can find no junior officers," the ship reported after a moment, sounding ever-so-slightly distressed.

"Go down the chain of command and let me know when you find someone who can be promoted to senior line officer in the event of catastrophic loss of life."

"I have three thousand nine hundred and seventeen individuals who fit those parameters."

"Is one of them alive?"

The ship was silent for a moment. "Yes."

I looked up at the amber-brown hull in surprise. "On this ship? Alive?"

"Yes."

"Where?" I checked the charge on my gun. Still above thirty percent. Good enough for government work.

"Second Sergeant Bradford Rios is in temporary stasis in medical hold twenty-nine B," the ship said.

"Is that the medical ward with a hole gaping into the vacuum of space?"

"Yes." There was a cricket chirp and the ship added, "Should I focus repair energies on that ship section?"

Ten days until we hit the critical point of maneuvers and were too close to the sun to escape.

"Sure. Repair away. Let me know when I can go rescue the new commanding officer."

Eight days later, I'd reached a wary understanding with the ship. It gave me correct information promptly, and I didn't stab it with an electroblade.

Electroblades are antique—kind of like me. Illegal just about everywhere I've been, but they're so rare that no one bothers to ask if you're carrying one. No sentient alive likes their flesh sliced while electricity floods their system. It's horribly painful, leaves scars that take decades to heal, and memories that never fade. Ask me how I know.

"Moira?" the ship said as I heaved another oversized Kanfir body into the airlock I was using as a dumping ground. Whatever they'd been feeding these boys, it was heavy in protein. Felin heavy bodies, all muscle and nice to look at—but pretty didn't stop bullets and it didn't make my disposal job any easier.

I slammed my fist against the lock plate. "Yes?"

"Medical hold twenty-nine B is secured and airtight. Would you like me to begin recovery of Second Sergeant Bradford Rios?"

"Yes please."

There was the cricket-like chirp I'd come to dread; the ship had found something that was going to cause an argument. "Second Sergeant Bradford Rios is under stasis lock for another ninety-two years, by the ship's working calendar."

I raised an eyebrow. "What for?"

"Treason, disobedience to a direct order, questioning a superior officer, blasphemy, violence, obstruction of justice, drunk or disorderly conduct, seventeen weapons infractions involving possession of a weapon or device of non-regulation origin, four weapons infractions involving discharge of a deadly weapon in a restricted area, fourteen weapons infractions involving failure to pass mandatory weapons inspections, and failure to complete a five kilometer run in under twenty minutes standard."

"Sounds like a real gem," I said. "Wake our boy up and let him know that he has been promoted to senior captain of the fleet."

"Admiral," the ship corrected. "But I do not believe the Second Sergeant can obtain the rank of Admiral with these charges against him. It's unprecedented."

"Did you find another beating heart on this tugboat?"

"Only you." The ship might have been a fleshy AI, but it made 'you' sound like the foulest curse word in the galaxy.

"Well then, it's me or your Boy Wonder for fleet admiral. Who would you rather answer to?"

"Beginning defrost sequence for Fleet Admiral Bradford Rios," the ship said quickly. "Estimated conscious alertness in thirty-eight minutes."

"Plenty of time."

I tidied up, dumped the bodies out the airlock, sorted hand weapons and other gewgaws I'd stripped off the dead, and wandered down to the newly restored medical bay.

I had to get myself one of these ships.

Self-repairing battleship? Be still my cold heart!

No matter how well-built a ship was, it eventually fell apart. Time destroyed things.

Most things.

I'd watched cultures rise and fall. Empires that came and went in the blink of an eye. Sometimes *really* in the blink of an eye. Most revolutions don't last more than a year or two, something historians forget because a year of anarchy always feels like an eternity.

The ship's medical hold was a barracks-style room with several dozen medical cots separated by membranous tissue the same amber-gold as the rest of the ship's interior.

Before alpha battalion had punched a hole in the side, there'd probably been blankets, and hand-held medical scanners, and the rest of the usual doctor paraphernalia. Now there was a Kanfir man in a clean engineering sergeant's uniform lying on a silver table, lips tinged blue.

"He is alive still, right? You didn't wake him up wrong?"

"The stasis chamber was below optimal temperature when the skitters retrieved the fleet admiral," the ship replied, "but he is within recovery range."

"Not brain dead?"

"There is a forty percent chance of brain damage with this procedure."

Not that the ship or I were likely to notice unless the damage left him drooling. Rios hadn't sounded like he was firing all pistons up top to begin with.

"Do you have a blanket or anything? He looks cold."

A cricket chirp. "Internal sensors cannot find anything similar to a blanket onboard. The stores room was completely destroyed, as were the barracks."

A lucky hit.

We'd caught the Kanfir ground forces sleeping in their bunks while the zoomies swatted at space gnats. Fly boys couldn't fight hand-to-hand like the infantry, not without a few drinks on them, and the loss of the entire infantry force of Kanfir in a single hit was more demoralizing to them than I'd expected.

"Fleet Admiral Rios is waking," the ship reported.

I turned to my new comrade at arms.

Time to play nice.

--------~~~\/\/~~~--------

Ford blinked his eyes at the harsh light. There was a little knick in the lamp cover. Either he'd been dragged out of stasis sleep on the *Subtle Queen* or someone had put up a fight going down. Icy nightmares clung in his mind. Shadows tugged at him even now—the last of the stasis drugs burning out of his body, he hoped. Stasis was hell.

"Wakey wakey, Admiral," a sardonic female voice said.

He turned, expecting to see one of her majesty's own medtechs, and instead saw a girl no more than twenty, wearing blood-red space armor and flipping a knife with a blade made of lightning. Fleet had clearly changed in the ninety-five years he'd spent tied in the shadows.

She winked at him. "How you feeling?"

Ford sat up slowly. The shadows tried to drag him down, but he made it upright. "Nauseous."

"I hear that happens after stasis."

He looked around the empty medical hold. "Doctor?"

The stranger shook her head. "Long story. Let's focus instead on the positive things, okay? Like your promotion."

Straight to her majesty's own slave mine. Ford grunted and watched the woman sheath her knife.

"You are the new fleet admiral." Her smile was cheerful and youthful, wholly at odds with her body language.

He smiled mirthlessly. "I wouldn't be promoted to anything in fleet unless everyone died, and even then it would be a long shot."

She nodded. "Funny story that. I'll tell you as we walk."

Ford tried to stand. The floor felt alien under his socks. "I need boots."

"What size?"

"Nine and three-quarters."

"Do you mind if they have blood on them?" She looked perfectly serious.

"Why not get them from ship stores?"

She wrinkled her nose. "There's a tiny problem with the ship stores."

"Queenie?" Ford said, calling for the ship.

"Fleet Admiral Rios?" the *Subtle Queen* replied evenly in Her Majesty's voice.

He shook his head. Unbelievable. "Queenie, may your humble penitent retrieve new boots and gear from the ship's stores?"

"Request denied," the Queen said.

"The ship doesn't have stores," the girl added. "There's now a gaping hole where the blankets used to be."

"And where are the Queen's Men?" Ford asked.

"Dead." The girl shrugged.

The cold shock rolled over him in a soft wave. It wasn't wholly unexpected. Only total devastation would bring the fleet to need him as a soldier of any kind. "What happened?"

Famine? Attack? Another internal coup between rival princesses?

"Me, mostly." The girl smiled. "You can call me Moira."

He stared at her childlike face. "You?"

"Like I said, long story. Now, let's walk over to the control room, and you can tell the ship to change course so we don't run into the sun. Then we'll have a nice long talk about astrochartography, political realities, and the chances of you living to see another meal. M'kay?"

Possibilities and theories free-wheeled through his mind until Ford caught hold of one reality. "We're diving into the sun?"

"Yes, and we have less than forty-eight hours to correct course before we're stuck with it. If you can't get the ship to obey, I'm going to need some time to find another way to reprogram this beast."

Ford stopped short. "You can't reprogram a celestial queen! She responds only to the voice of Her Majesty or the Queen's Men who fight for her life and honor!"

Moira looked unmoved. "I know where the brain center is. Talk the ship into changing course, or your queen gets a lobotomy."

Ford stared at her. "Are all women like you?"

"All the women you need to worry about."

--------∿∿∿∿--------

The former sergeant wasn't happy with his sudden change of rank. His body language shifted as we walked down the deserted halls, still splashed with dried blood. In the medical hold he'd been depressed but mostly relaxed, reacting slowly. The further we walked, the tenser he became. Muscles bunched up in his shoulders. His fists curled. His stride became a defiant march past the field of battle now a week old.

"They're all dead?"

"It was the Kanfir or the Euonians." I shrugged. "That's the thing about wars. People die."

He shook his head. "It wasn't war. Her Majesty's children required new suns to graze near. The fleet was called to search the star paths for the coming swarm."

"Swarm? Like... insect swarm?"

He frowned. "Know you nothing of the Kanfir?"

"Hyper-violent male race with enslaved females kept locked on their home planet. You guys come in, kill everyone, and then abandon the systems you've destroyed."

He stopped walking and stared.

I rolled my eyes. "I've seen it done in Gretchuia and Rison. Don't deny it. I saw the senate house of Dreul when you were done in the Gretchuia system. There was nothing left. Even the stones were dust."

"Because Her Majesty ordered the place prepared for her brood!" he protested. "Her Majesty called. We cannot disobey her will."

"You need a new government," I said.

He shook his head violently this time. "No. No. You mistake me. Us. Her Majesty owns us. We are the Queen's Men. We cannot disobey. Not 'We don't think about disobeying', or 'We don't want to disobey', or 'We all agree with Her Majesty'. We *cannot* go against her. She is the Life Giver and the Life Taker. There is no way but hers. When she wishes to lay a clutch, we obey and clear land, and now her daughters seek to swarm, to take suns of their own. We obey or we die."

"Or you obey and still die." I smiled. "Looks like a lose-lose situation all around." I led him to the control room. "Does this whole queen business mean I can't take over the ship at all, ever?"

"The ship is the *Subtle Queen*. It is a piece of Her Majesty, and extension of her will and dominion."

"I'm not actually hearing a no here."

The sergeant stalked over to the control console and stared. "I was never trained for this."

"No worries. I know what I'm doing." I showed him how to call up the screen and set various coordinates.

"I should take us home," he said.

I shook my head. "Bad idea. At home you still have a prison sentence to live out. Let's go somewhere fun. Escinia is nice this time of year. Or the Sertian colonies. I hear they're making great progress with the swamp plagues. We can go, find new jobs, loiter on a beach somewhere, make new friends... It'll be great!"

He stared at her. "These are not places I have ever heard of."

"Again, no worries. When I was growing up I'd never heard of them either."

I gave him the coordinates to Sertian space. They were a disorganized group with multiple governments on each of their three settled planets and they promised to have an interesting future. It was somewhere a person could get lost in the tides of humanity.

The sergeant sat reluctantly, then turned. "Where were you born? Far from here? On Dreul perhaps?"

"I was born in San Francisco on this cute little planet called Earth."

He frowned. "That is an Elder Planet, one long forgotten, the Star Paths to it closed."

I shrugged. "I didn't say I was born recently. I mean, when I was a kid the big excitement was that man had walked on the moon. Interstellar travel was a fiction then." I snorted in amusement. "I thought driving eight hours to see my grandma on holidays was a big adventure because we crossed a desert."

"But... you're a child!" He held his hand near my head. "You're not grown yet."

I smiled. "I'm short. I'm not a kid."

"You are still young."

"Younger than the universe maybe, but not as young as I look." I sat down in the first officer's chair. "I visited Dreul when they were building the senate house. That was nearly three hundred years ago. I remember the system was found by a probe from Xalian. It was all over the news for months. New world found! Habitable planet!" I waved my hands, feigning enthusiasm. "Everyone was so excited and then there were arguments over whether the Xalian river gods approved of Dreul. Once they found the gold river it was fine, of course. Obviously a heaven planet. People rioted for a chance to go. The murder rate sextupled overnight. Crazy times."

Rios sat beside me in the captain's chair. "You learned all this as a child?"

"I lived all that as an adult. An old woman. Very old." I shrugged.

"You don't look old."

"Aging is the decay of telomeres. Your body stops replicating the cells correctly. Mutations take over. You fall apart. You die. I don't. I have no cellular mutations."

"That's very strange."

"Truly freakish," I agreed.

"Impossible," the ship chimed in. "There is no similar anomaly on record."

I looked at the amber ceiling. "How many times was I shot during the initial assault on this vessel?"

"Nineteen direct hits recorded," the ship said petulantly.

"Do we need to have another talk about behaving?" I flipped open my electroknife.

There was a cricket chirp from the ship. "No."

"Didn't think so."

I smiled for the Kanfir's benefit. "Don't worry about it. I'm a freak. I was born this way. I'd say I'll die this way, but, well, that'd be a lie."

"It seems many things in life are lies," he murmured.

For a moment I wondered if I'd have to use the electro-blade on him to get him to cooperate, but abruptly he placed both hands on the console.

He smiled at me, a toothy thing that hardened his eyes. "And you'll show me the universe," he said.

My own smile stretched wider in response. "I'll show you the universe."

"Then I'd better turn us around."

As he reset the course, I sighed and felt the tension in my shoulders release. I had all of eternity left at my disposal; might as well make it worthwhile.

HERE SHE LIES

Perhaps the dress was a little much. It was a yearly party to celebrate the company and most other people had come in the same clothes they'd worn last time. Some had even come straight from work.

Esana paused outside the main ballroom and looked at the gold-tinted mirror. The white dress had been bought years ago on a whim, shimmering white with a teardrop neckline that clasped around her neck and plummeted down in a slinky slide of snowy crystals with a generous scoop to display her cleavage. It had sat at the back of her closet all this time and it wasn't going to be too many more years before eating too much at her desk and forgetting to workout made the dress unwearable.

She twisted. If she looked better than everyone else at the party, so be it. That was the price they would have to pay for not putting in the effort.

A loud laugh broke out and then thunderous applause as the lights died and the main entertainment began. A concert with live performers. The room felt crowded even from the wrong side of the door.

Come this way, the stairs whispered. *Up on the balcony. Away from the crowds. You'll be safe here. No one will notice.*

It was a good idea. After all, she'd made an appearance, greeted everyone who needed to see her in attendance, and there was no one saving a seat on the main floor. On an empty balcony she could enjoy the concert and then escape as soon as everything was over.

The long dress pooled around her feet and made her take the stairs with a slow, regal step that would have made her co-workers laugh. Elegant and beautiful were not words they'd ever apply to her. She lifted her chin and pretended to be a princess, sweeping up the staircase... But to what?

A love? How dull.

A secret meeting? Too work-ish.

An intelligence conference? Yes, that would be where she was if she were a princess, taking intelligence reports and spinning those reports into actionable plans to save her people or expand the trade routes.

"Thank the stars for marketing." *There, but for the grace of quick thinking, go I.*

She reached the top of the stairs and relaxed a little, listening to the murmur of voices. The boxes to the right were all full, but there were three to the left, close to the service elevator and the back stairs, that sounded like they were empty. Smiling, she turned toward them.

There was a crack of gunfire as the cymbals crashed inside the concert hall.

Esana froze, listening, but there were no screams. Maybe it had been her imagination. A drum beat that sounded too much like her neighborhood on a bad night.

When she was confident no one was screaming for help, she moved forward again.

The service door slammed open and Lev Sevastionovich stumbled through, glassy-eyed. He focused on her and sucked air through his teeth. "What are you doing here?"

"I... was coming to see if everyone had drinks," Esana lied.

He had his hand up under his shirt.

"Can I get you anything, Sevastionovich?" She used the politest term she could, not the indifferent Mr. Aleksiev or the too familiar Lev, but a name that recognized his place in the company. "Wine perhaps?"

"No. I'm fine."

He pushed away from the service door and all but fell through the door to the private balcony.

Esana hurried as fast as the skirt would allow. "Sir—"

He was waiting in the door frame. "Leave."

"I can—"

"Leave. I want to be alone." It hardly took an empathic skill to feel the injury radiating on his side or realize he was moments away from passing out. "As you say, sir." She bowed her head and turned away, an obedient drone.

The door closed behind her and she counted to ten, long enough for Sevastionovich to find his seat, and then she felt his mind crumble into darkness. He was going to die of blood loss on the balcony of a company party and the day would be forever marred.

Inexcusable.

Thankfully the company had been renting the hall for every major event since she'd joined six years ago, and in that time no one had ever moved the first-aid kit. She found it and checked the contents. Bandages, a patch to improve blood clotting times, a rehydration and antibiotic patch, and at the very bottom a pack of stimulant pills that could wake the dead. Not even expired.

But no cleansing wipes.

She'd need the wine after all.

Sweeping the train of her skirt into her hands she used the folds of the white gown to hide the med kit while she carried the wine in her other hand. She even rapped her knuckles on the door in case someone checked the cameras later. "Mister Aleksiev? Sevastionovich?" The door opened under slight pressure.

Music swelled around, a grand triumphant crescendo as the door snicked shut, locking her in the gloom of the private box.

She twitched the curtains back enough to give her a sliver of light and surveyed the patient.

Sevastionovich was passed out in the first seat, his shirt still in his hand. At least he'd managed to get that off before he collapsed. There was blood pooling on his dark pants, but that would probably go unnoticed.

Esana uncorked the wine, splashed it on a sanitary gauze and washed the wound. A simple graze. So the collapse was less likely to be from blood loss and more from shock. That happened sometimes. Being shot was never an easy thing.

As the orchestra played a running melody with angry horns blaring behind them, Esana cleaned the wound and applied the patches. She put the pills on Sevastionovich's tongue and tipped wine into his mouth. She checked his pulse.

It was only when she stood up again that she saw the smear of red blood across her torso. Nothing else had gone right all day, but at least she'd been right about the dress: she'd never be able to wear it again.

The door handle rattled.

Sevastionovich groaned, turning his head away from the sound.

Explaining this would require getting the boss involved. It would mean meetings, paperwork, and an unpleasant evening when her job depended on everything being pleasant. On the other hand, lying required only that she put her dignity on the line. It wasn't worth much anyway. She grabbed Sevastionivich's jacket and pulled it on, then pulled the pin from her hair and let it fall loose.

There was a knock at the door.

"Coming!" She giggled as she draped Sevastionovich's shirt over the bandages. "A moment, please!"

Putting on the smile she usually reserved for lucrative clients, she opened the door just enough to put one jacket-clad shoulder out and beam at the visitors.

Cecil stared at her.

"Cecil! How are you? I was..." Esana paused and looked back over her shoulder. "Um... diverted." She giggled again.

A bright flush of second-hand embarrassment and jealousy rushed through Cecil.

"Can I help you with something?" She batted her eyes at the two men in dark security suits standing behind him. "Is something wrong?"

"Ma'am," one of the men took off his cap, "we're with the portside security force. Have you seen anyone with a gunshot this evening?"

"A... a gunshot?" She widened her eyes in shock. "No. Why... Cecil, is everything perfectly all right?" She pushed the door wide, hugging the jacket over the bloodstain on her dress. "If anything ruins this party we will both be looking for work and I won't be giving you a good recommendation." The anger burned at the top of her mind, keeping out an intrusion from the men, although they didn't feel like empaths.

Cecil shook his head. "Nothing's wrong! I did nothing wrong."

"Someone was shot outside," the security officer said.

Esana raised her eyebrows in confused alarm. "Who?"

The security guards exchanged glances. They shared a mutual concern for privacy with a pressing need to find their victim. "There's a unregistered intelligence operative who came on planet this week," one said finally. "We were tracking them and successfully shot them, but didn't render them—"

"Dead?" Esana finished for him.

All three men were shocked.

"We weren't able to slow the intruder," the second guard said.

There was another exchange of glances.

"Ma'am, we need to inspect the box," the second security guard said.

Esana took a deep, heaving breath that made the crystals of her dress sparkle as her breasts rose and fell. "Um..." *Thank you acting classes where I learned to blush on command.* "...Could you perhaps, give us a moment? We're..." She laughed. "...I mean I'm not..."

She cleared her throat and looked at the ground in embarrassment.

Cecil turned bright red. "It's all well, Esana. Who—who are you here with?"

"Ah..." That was a little trickier.

If she could keep Cecil from knowing then tomorrow wouldn't be nearly as large as a disaster.

Of course, if the guards walked in and saw the blood, the troubles she'd have would include jail time. Esana started to close the door. It caught on something. She looked up at a strong, tanned hand, and the unbuttoned cuffs of an expensive white shirt.

"She is with me," Sevastionovich said.

Lev leaned against the doorframe to keep from pitching forward. The stimulants the girl had slipped him had gotten him moving, but his head was still swimming. He looked down. There was little to see but lush brown hair, his jacket hiding a beautifully sculpted body, and a white dress that should have looked tacky but was instead contributing to his inability to breathe properly.

As soon as the guards were gone, he'd have to figure out how this had happened.

"Sevastionovich!" Cecil looked up at him in shock. "Esana!"

So that was her name. It suited her.

"I can explain!" Esana said breathlessly, leaning forward just enough to rivet everyone's attention, burning away all the oxygen. "Um... Where do I start?" She looked up at him through long black lashes, eyes filled with admiration he knew she didn't feel.

"Start at the beginning, my charm. That summer we met."

She laughed happily. "Of course! Lev and I knew each other from the Port Royale Resort. I worked there over the summer and his family always vacationed there." She snuck him another appreciative glance. "He would be swimming when I came to change the flowers every afternoon. Even then he was handsome." Her eyes caressed him shamelessly.

The security guard pulled out a notebook. "Do you recall the address?"

"Mmm." Esana closed her eyes. "I forget the house number, but the door was yellow, and the house was blue, with a white roof. It was on Forsythe Lane along the western shore of the peninsula."

Lev stared. That was the family's summer house. He could remember the smell of honeysuckle on the evening tide.

"There was a smell of honeysuckle, and in the evening there was woodsmoke from the pizza grill." Her smile was a joyful indulgence, as if she were recalling her happiest memory.

"You said you didn't know him!" Cecil complained.

Esana dipped her eyes and her cheeks turned rosy. "I didn't really introduce myself properly. It wasn't a formal meeting. But, you know how it is in the summer time. You meet so many interesting people, and one thing led to another. I didn't think I'd see him again, but when we saw each other the other day there was..." She paused to look up at him again.

Lev looked down at her and raised an eyebrow.

"Chemistry," she said.

Antagonism would have been more accurate, but hate was a sort of chemistry too.

"An indescribable something. We wound up talking and reconnecting." She shrugged elegantly.

Cecil crossed his arms.

"You heard nothing?" the security officer asked.

"Oh, I heard plenty." Esana's tone was suggestive. "But with the orchestra and other sounds I'm afraid I didn't hear anything outside our little reunion. Did you, Lev?"

His smile this time was real. "I heard many things, my charm, but none of them were gunshots. Mostly moans." He drew the word out to feel her reaction, but there was nothing.

This Esana was cold as winter water under her sultry smiles. Unruffled by the guards or the blood.

Lev gathered his strength and moved an arm to catch the strange woman before she could run away. Under the jacket he felt a wet, sticky patch along her abdomen. Blood. His. That complicated matters. He couldn't very well send her back to the party like this.

"A problem?" the security guard asked.

"There's, ah, something different about the dress." Lev looked down at Esana.

Her smile could have ended wars. Or started them.

"There was a zipper there earlier this evening. Before our little reunion party."

"Ah." The security guard closed his notebook. "You've been very helpful," he said sarcastically.

"I'm so sorry, officer," Esana said, pulling away from Lev's touch. "Can I do more? I know this building very well. There's a third-story exit on the south side that connects to the restaurant next door. You can take the stairs there directly to the subway entrance. We use it all the time to get prominent guests in and out. I'll show you."

Lev pinched the fabric on her dress between his fingers, trying to keep her from running away.

She reached for the jacket as if she was going to forget the broken zipper and hurry to help.

"I know the entrance," Cecil said. He gave Esana a hurt look. "I'd be happy to show them."

"You're such a delight, Cecil."

The smile Esana gave him cured the man's melancholy. Poor fool thought he had a chance with her.

Lev found it very unpleasant. "Cecil, could you call us a car? I'm…"—he gave Esana the slow once over she'd treated him to—"…interested in going somewhere quieter."

Esana's surface thoughts found this perfectly agreeable, but there was no attraction there. No interest in him. Her pulse didn't leap at the chance to take advantage of him in any way. It was like she had a to-do list and somewhere at the bottom had found the words 'Save Lev' and decided to get it finished before she went home to wash her hair.

"My treasure, you don't mind going somewhere else tonight, do you?" he asked.

She stood on tiptoe so she was almost close enough to kiss. "How could I object?"

"I'll have the car ready in a moment," Cecil said quickly.

"I'll get the rest of the wine," Esana said. She nodded politely to the officers and slipped back into the darkness of the balcony.

"Cecil," Lev said, "I am leaving early so there will be no gossip. Do you understand?"

The man's eyes went wide with fright. "Naturally, Sevastionovich. No one will hear of this from me."

"Thank you, I appreciate discretion. This really was only a reunion."

Esana came back with the half-empty wine bottle and walked down the stairs with him, one hand pressing the jacket close around her.

She climbed into the car without a word and sat stoically beside him for the short drive back to his family's residence.

It was only when they were inside and the doors were closed that her sweet, lovestruck expression slipped away and the real Esana appeared.

She pulled off the jacket and hung it over the back of a chair. "Will that be all for the evening, Sevastionovich?"

"No." Lev sat on the edge of the table, not trusting himself to the comfort of a chair. "Tell me why you did this."

She raised an eyebrow. "It's my job to see the annual party runs smoothly. Finding the president's son passed out or dead from blood loss would be an unacceptable outcome for the evening. Now you're home safe and my job is done."

"What about the security officers? Or the gunshot?"

"What about them?"

It was his turn to be surprised. There was nothing behind her words. Not a single flicker of emotion. "Don't you have questions?"

"Sevastionovich, I know your record. You were a traveling teacher and humanitarian since college. Do you know what's required for a teaching accreditation on this planet? An empath score of Skilled or higher.

"The highest national export for our solar system is empaths trained in espionage of one form or another. The most common cover for an espionage agent from this region is teacher. The most common plot line for a romance story for the past nineteen years has been a Returned Spy Finds Love. For nearly two decades this has dominated the national consciousness. Anyone with the ability to add two and two together knows what happened to you.

"You were an empath, you were offered a job, it worked out until they remembered you're a dirty foreigner, and now you're home where your family name can protect you."

"That is... an interesting view."

"And," she continued, "the bullet was poorly aimed but managed to take out whatever tracker you'd been tagged with, which is either very good luck or very good planning. Either way, you'll live through the night." There was no hint she cared if he lived or died.

"There's nothing you want to know?"

"I'm not paid to ask questions, Sevastionovich."

That name again. Sevastionovich. Son of Sevastion. Owned and belonging to Sevastion Aleksiev. "Lev," he said. "Call me Lev. And at least let me have your dress cleaned."

"I have a uterus. I know how to get blood out of clothes."

"So practical. Do you plan to go home like this?"

She glanced down at her clothes and there was a hint of consternation.

"Allow me to offer you something to change into, my treasure."

"I doubt you have anything in your closet my size, my heart." The look she gave him was sharp and biting. "Now, if you have no further need of me, Sevastionovich, I'll be going."

"Lev." He stood and moved to block the exit. "Stay. Change. We need to talk."

Her dark eyes studied him but gave nothing away.

It had been years since he'd met someone so collected and unreadable. If he ever had. "You realize that if any of those men were empaths, they would have read your lie."

"What lie?" Esana radiated innocence. He could feel it, the complete and perfect belief that she had not lied. "I worked at the resort. Your family summered there. The guests flirted with the staff all the time. I'm certain that, at some point, you kissed a dark-haired girl surrounded by the smell of honeysuckle."

"True, but it wasn't you."

"Can you prove that?" Esana tilted her head and widened her eyes. It was a very calculated gesture, but it looked natural. If he couldn't feel her thinking about it, he would have been fooled.

He nodded. "How did you know the house color?"

"There's a picture of your family in front of it in your brother's office and I have an excellent memory."

"The girl I kissed?"

"Over eighty percent of the female wait staff at the resort had dark hair. The likelihood of a neighborhood busybody noticing you kissing one would be over seventy-two percent. If the security officers ask, they'll find a witness."

Lev took her hand. "So calculated. Come here. You can't go home like that. Someone will notice you leaving here covered in blood."

There was a mute resistance and then she followed along begrudgingly to his rooms. "I'm sure I can find a shirt you can wear. I'll have the dress laundered discreetly."

"I can handle it."

"Without anyone noticing the blood on the front?" Doubtful.

"I wasn't going to wear the dress again anyway."

He looked at her again. "That would be a shame, my charm."

Anger flared behind her blank eyes. "Feel free to drop the act, Sevastionovich."

"Lev," he insisted as he held out a white shirt. "You can change in the washroom."

"You're too kind, sir." She gave him a mocking bow and sashayed through his room.

The door clicked shut between them and he heard the soft whisper of cloth across skin. He kept his thoughts obscured. "You're not an empath, are you, Miss Esana?"

"No." Quick and cutting. "I'd have significantly better job options if I were gifted."

"And, your lover, how will you explain tonight to them?"

"There's no need to explain to anyone. I'm comfortably single." The door opened. "How will you explain to your girlfriend?"

He raised an eyebrow, mimicking her earlier expression. "I haven't had one in the better part of a year. So, like you, no explanation is necessary. You are certain you have no talents?"

"My mind is dead as a tree's," she said without emotion. "I have it on good authority that I'm an evolutionary failure. But everyone in my family is like this. Genetics." She shrugged.

"No mind is dead. Some are quieter than others, but I should be able to get some reading off you."

She stared deep into his eyes, letting the silence fill the room around them. "Why? I feel nothing, so there is nothing to read."

Lev smiled. That had been a lie. There'd been a tug to her words, a hint of emotion. She was hiding something from him very, very well. "You're an interesting person, my charm."

"Esana!"

"Lev."

Her eyes closed for a moment and the anger he should have felt wasn't there. "Sir, must you insist on being informal?"

He tilted his head to the side as he looked her up and down, long tan legs bare beneath his white shirt, a hint of white lace corsetry hidden behind his buttons, her dark hair tussled and wavy. "Under the circumstances, my light, I think formality would be rather coarse. This is not a business transaction."

"It's not a lover's exchange either."

"Perhaps a simple moment shared between friends, then."

"Where's my purse?" Esana muttered. She hurried back to the living room, moving faster than he could keep up.

By the time he turned the corner, she was knotting a scarf around her waist and rolling up the sleeves. She pirouetted for him. "Thoughts?"

He smiled, letting admiration run under his words. "You look divine, Esana. Stunningly beautiful."

"Hmm." Her eyes narrowed. "I was going for casual fun at the club."

"Only at a very nice club."

She lifted a shoulder in a shrug. "I have a stable job. I can afford the good clubs sometimes. Is there anything further, Se—" Her lips twisted at his look. "Sir?"

"You are certain you're loyal to no one?"

"Only to your father's company, sir."

"I don't need to write a thank you note to anyone?"

"No one at all, sir." She walked towards the door.

"I'll see you tomorrow?"

Her steps slowed only by a fraction. "If you're well enough for work, sir."

The door opened and his brother walked in, a woman hanging on his arm.

"Sevastionovich-ile!" Esana stepped back quickly.

"Esana?" His brother looked her up and down. "I thought you were still at the concert."

"Oh, I, ah, spilled some wine on my gown." She held up the folded mess. "I was going to go home, but your brother saw me and offered me a chance to change. Here."

That was a terrible lie and they both knew it. Thankfully his brother was more than a little drunk. Issyk waved a hand. "Stay! Stay, Esana and meet..." He peered at the woman on his arm.

"Bettani." She giggled, her thoughts bouncing higher than the clouds on whatever cocktail of drugs and liquor his brother had provided.

"Bettani!" Issyk shouted. "We will have a party here! Just us lovers."

Esana was already shaking her head. "It's not like that, Sevastionovich-ile. Your brother and I are not—"

Issyk grabbed her by the arm and pushed her towards Lev. "Stay. Make my brother smile."

Anger touched Esana's thoughts.

"Give me a moment," Lev murmured in her ear. "Can you take Bettani home?"

"Yes." Esana's words were tight with frustration.

He ran a hand along her shoulder, trying to whisper calming thoughts to her mind.

The response was a stinging retort that shocked him.

Mind dead?

Not even close.

ACKNOWLEDGMENTS

Many years ago, back when I remembered to check writing forums daily, there was a tiny portion of the internet called The Slacker's Corner. In The Slacker's Corner, a group of very busy people who never really learned to slack at all got together, talked about writing, posted challenges, and exchanged ideas. It was the birth place of characters like Ice Rus from *The Boy Named No* and the first audience for *Red Planet Refugees*. If it weren't for those authors staying up late to chase their dreams, this collection wouldn't exist, so thank you to all of them for their love and encouragement.

ABOUT THE AUTHOR

LIANA BROOKS is an American author who writes science fiction and sci-fi romance for people who like fast ships, big guns, witty one-liners, and happy endings. She enjoys writing science fiction in every form, from sprawling space operas (*Fleet of Malik*) to the antics of a superhero family (*Heroes and Villains*), as well as paranormal romances (*All I Want For Christmas*).

When she's not exploring the sprawling realms of fiction, she is a busy mother of four, traveler, language learner, and eclectic hobbyist who enjoys everything from woodworking and photography to cooking and embroildery. She lives somewhere between the bookshelves, quilts, and canvases with her wonderful husband, their beautiful pets, and all the children that want to be at home right now.

You can find Liana online at www.lianabrooks.com, and on Twitter as @LianaBrooks.

ALSO BY LIANA BROOKS

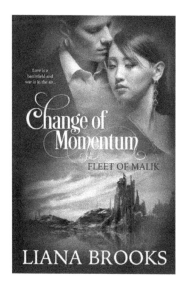

CHANGE OF MOMENTUM
Fleet Of Malik

Love is a battlefield,
and war is in the air...

Available from all major online retailers in print
and ebook.

CHANGE OF MOMENTUM
CHAPTER 1

THE HYPERTRAM FROM RYUN TO KYTAN WAS RUNNING three minutes late, a silver-blue moonbeam racing across the golden desert. It was one of the little inef-ficiencies that made Malcolm Long hate ground travel. That and the other passengers, of course.

Waving off an offer of food from the refreshment cart, he settled into a seat on the port side of the tram and bullishly stared out the window as they rushed across the barren rock between the city-states.

High overhead, a shining Koenig-1-11 caught the sunlight as it turned for a landing in Dreyun to the north.

Long's lips twitched into a frown as he pulled out his ever-present palm pad to take notes. The one-elevens were supposed to be phased out by now. Blue Sky Air Transport had been sold off six weeks ago to Lethe, and Lethe was replacing the one-elevens with the Koenig-360, a plane with a fabulous interior and fuel consumption that made him wince.

He assumed that was why Lethe had contacted his offices two days ago to request this meeting. They were paying for his travel, and had offered a consulting fee that was generous without being obscene.

The whole set-up made the hair on the back of his neck stand up.

Senior engineers at small research firms did not generally get attention like this. Especially since he hadn't published anything in over a year. His team had been busy, and he'd been juggling too many projects to finish anything of substance.

If this was about the Koenig-360s, he could handle the matter in a couple of weeks. If it wasn't…

An old fear clawed up his throat.

For a moment the crowded tram was silent, devoid of oxygen, cold as the dark between stars. Memories of pain and rage threatened to destroy him. His heart raced as he fought the fear. Pulled it under. Drowned it in the memories of today.

That had been another life.

Another name.

A time of power and cruelty—because the two always went hand in hand. But it was the past. He'd left the islands and there was no way Lethe could know who he had been.

Lips twitching into a grim smile, he checked his watch as the rocks gave way to the cultivated terraces of Kytan. Red rock formations ringed what were laughably called terraformed plateaus, bordered first with grain crops dividing the desert from the cultivated countryside, and then the land rippled inward past pools of pale pink water lilies, and into a sea of blue-green iridescent irises that sparkled like a dragonfly's wing.

Kytan was famous for the blooms that appeared for six weeks during the height of the Descent wedding season. Right now, the city-state was overflowing with tourists who wanted to wander the parks and young couples taking engagement photos for next summer.

The tram went straight to the hanging gardens hiding the terraced buildings at the heart of the city. The air was cooler there under the shade of the vines, effervescent with the scent of falling water, and the crowd hurried past him to catch the city transports while he walked, briefcase in hand, along a stream-lined road.

The artisinal waterway was filled with silvery-blue fish that swam through the sun-dappled water against the current flowing down from the step pyramids at the city center.

The original home of the Imperial Governor of Malik IV, designed to match the legendary summer palace of Emperor Insei Qui the Third, the pyramids in the center of the city were an architectural wonder, covered in towering waterfalls and fronds and vines of greenery. Great stone mountains built in the desert plain and covered with a deep green jungle, with flowers of brilliant white and pink burning along the branches like captured stars. The whole city sparkled like the dead emperor's scepter, exactly as the first arrivals from the old Empire had hoped.

"A thousand years of freedom and still we bow," Long murmured to himself. He couldn't remember the rest of the poem now, but he remembered when he'd first heard it, in the halls at school spoken by a girl who'd both captivated and challenged him.

She would have appreciated the architecture of Kytan. Probably had the opportunity to, considering her family and wealth.

Or perhaps not.

With the powerful families on the first continent, it all depended on who you knew and who you were allied with.

The Longs were a small family with no allies, unless his mother's book club friends counted, which he personally didn't feel they needed to. A family name, the right genes, a pittance of an inheritance, and an acre of land somewhere out in the wilds between city-states. It had been enough to get his family off the islands along the edge of the second continent and earn him a scholarship to the most prestigious university, but it wouldn't keep him alive if the Lethes wanted him dead.

Especially not here in their capital city.

"I suppose I should have asked for a bodyguard," he muttered to himself. One of the lab interns had the height and reach to be a good shield—but also the personality of a frightened rabbit, which might have made the graceless man more a liability than an asset.

Long followed the streams to the step pyramid and walked up the wide steps until he reached the main entrance. The arched glass doors opened into a chilled atrium, where the light passing through the waterfalls outside rippled and splashed over the dark marble floor.

Jewel-colored hummingbirds zipped past, chasing each other to the background music of a drowsy orchestral melody.

He felt he should applaud the theatrics, but restrained himself instead to a small half-smile.

The Lethes didn't sound like the kind of people who would enjoy his sense of humor.

A man in the Lethe colors of deep purple and slate gray approached him, white hair slicked back to an opalescent sheen. "May I help you, sir?"

"Doctor Malcolm Long. I have an appointment."

"Certainly, sir. If you'll please follow me."

He gestured to a bank of black lifts behind a discreet marble reception desk. The greeter stepped around and peered at a screen that Long had the good manners not to peek at.

Or at least not to get caught peeking at.

"You're a few minutes early, sir," the greeter said, glancing up at him with a moue of censure.

"My apologies. I have the day free if you would like me to wait." He must have rushed. And now I look too eager, he berated himself. On time was on time. Eager looked weak. Late was disrespectful. It was these little social mores that kept the culture of Descent afloat.

The greeter shook his head. "No, I apologize, sir. The computer recalculated the time based on the tram delay. You have arrived on schedule, but a few minutes later would have been acceptable as well. If you'll take lift number seven, sir, it will take you to your meeting room."

That wasn't much information to go on.

Today's invitation had come from Lethe Corp, but without a signature. It was one of the annoying habits of the business people on the first continent that they used to keep their rivals guessing. Not knowing who he was meeting with meant he couldn't study or prepare for the meeting, not unless he wanted to study the several hundred middle managers, division leads, and board members.

He stepped into the mirrored elevator and tried to avoid glancing at his reflection, afraid he'd catch himself glaring and remember what a bad idea it was to get caught up in the machinations of political fanatics.

The mirror image glared back anyway.

For good reason, too; he should have worn a touch of Lethe purple somewhere to show a willingness to work together. The dark gray suit with a white shirt was a little too neutral. Long jerked the edge of one cuff straighter, an expression of annoyance tugging at his lips. He suppressed that too. This was a stupid risk to take. But declining, he suspected, would have proven fatal.

The door to the lift opened to a long, wide room with a row of slit windows overlooking the city. The only furniture was a white stone desk, carved to look like it had grown out of the stone floor. The walls were lined with silent waterfalls that pooled around the edge of the room, filled with small green reeds that had either been genetically engineered for the poor lighting or were fake; he couldn't tell at this distance.

At the desk, a woman was silhouetted by the window light, her pale hair swept up into a coiling, sleek up-do and held in place by a pin with a dripping chain of amethysts that matched her silk shirt. She was framed by the jungle outside, a pale diamond in the city of jewels. The effect was stunning, albeit contrived.

Long waited in front of the lift for her to acknowledge him as a dark suspicion formed.

Several minutes crept by before the woman finished her work, turned off her screen and stood. Recessed lights in the ceiling turned on as she moved, spotlighting Sonya Lethe, the sole heir of the Lethe fortune.

Fear crawled down his spine with cold fingers.

This is what a fish feels like when it sees a shark. I always wondered.

"Doctor Long, please, come in," she said from behind the desk. "I'm delighted you could make time in your schedule to come to Kytan today."

"The delight is mine," he said, repeating the proper polite phrasing. "I've been looking for an excuse to come to Kytan."

"Wedding season," Sonya said with a slink of a smile. "Is there someone you were hoping to show the flowers to?"

"Much to my mother's dismay, there is not."

Sonya walked around her desk and perched on the front edge. "Yes, she is Nettie Amherst of the Northland Amhersts, isn't she?"

"The last of that line to bear the Amherst name, yes." Sonya had done her homework, both a threat and a show of strength. Or maybe she thought it put them on equal footing. After all, any schoolchild raised on Descent could name the Lethe heirs back to the first ship.

"Perhaps your future spouse will see fit to revive the name. Long is...." She pursed her lips as she looked him up and down in an appraising way. "...Perhaps a little generic?"

He let the insult pass with a smile. "My father says it's a dialect word from the Grizhjan System meaning 'dragon'. I make it a rule never to argue translations with a linguist."

Sonya laughed. It was a calculated move, the arch of her neck, the degree of her smile, the uplift of her breasts, all mathematically designed to hide the fact that the muscles around her eyes never moved. She wasn't amused, she was manipulating him.

There were few things in the world that felt worse.

Long waited her out. Social graces did not require him to laugh along with her, so he didn't.

"Doctor Long, you look so grim. I do not like grim faces at business."

"Forgive me, Miss Lethe, I wasn't sure what response you anticipated. My name is not often a topic of conversation."

She smiled with an apologetic head tilt. "Engineers. You're always so delightfully focused, aren't you?"

"It's been mentioned before."

"Excellent." Sonya nodded. "Focus, I believe, is something this project needs. Please, take a seat." She brushed her hand along a control set in the stone desk and a chair materialized to one side, perfectly set to give the occupant a view of both the city and Sonya at their best angles.

Long regarded the chair with quiet suspicion. It was a trap, that much was obvious, but he wasn't sure exactly what kind.

Days like this, he thought about throwing it all away and moving back to the islands.

But then he'd never be able to fly again. And flying again was the only reason he kept breathing. Everything else was lost to him, but maybe, one day, he could reclaim the sky.

"It's quite safe," Sonya assured him as she took her own seat behind the desk. "The matter transporter is something new our research and development team is working on. It could replace all travel one day."

All the more reason to hate it.

Aloud he said, "I'd heard of research along those lines, but I thought we were decades away from a breakthrough." Unless someone was getting tech from the space fleet that had landed on the third continent. He, like most people, wasn't privy to the fine details of the treaty the planetary representative had signed with them, but he felt certain the tech they'd brought with them was off limits.

"This can only move objects a few feet. But it is fun to bring a chair in from the closet at the touch of a button. There's an awe factor I appreciate." She sat back with a smug smile, the empress on her throne.

"I can imagine." He took a seat and dutifully surveyed the view of the city.

Sonya sat in the chair across from him, blonde hair framed by the shimmering blue flowers. "Tell me, Doctor Long, do you have your father's gift for languages?"

The question blindsided him and he let a frown slip. "No. Some, I suppose. I speak all the regional cants of the first and second continents and can read the Journals Of Discovery in the original Imperial Script, but that's a talent any well-educated person on Descent can boast of." Especially since the dialects only changed a handful of slang terms between all of them. Calling them languages was a bit of an insult to the idea of diversity, really.

"You claim to have no gift for languages, but you broke the hardest cipher we know while at university." She laughed. "What a shame everyone isn't as lacking in gifts."

"Ah," he said, shrugging one shoulder in dismissal. "Cryptography is a ghost from my misguided youth." And he hadn't broken the cipher alone. The key to the whole thing had been in an obscure text his classmate had found.

Technically, he should have credited her, but that would have required finding her after the move to Descent, and he hadn't had the resources. And she was unlikely to want to speak to him ever again anyway.

"I work exclusively in aeronautical science now. That was why I thought you'd called me in, to solve the fuel efficiency problems with the Koenig-360?" He let the opening dangle.

Sonya waved the comment aside. "Planes are relics. We can burn all the fuel we want. In a few years the new matter transporters will be the foundation of Lethe's transportation division. Let the Koenigs fly. This project is much more time sensitive." She held up a datcube, black and small enough to be concealed in his fist.

Long raised an eyebrow in question.

"This belonged to one of my employees. At the time of his death he had no heir, so the data became company property."

How convenient for Lethe.

"My techs have been able to decrypt a portion of the data on here, but the rest is beyond them. We've applied to other experts Lethe already has a working relationship with, but neither were able to decrypt it. Both experts mentioned you." She held the datcube out to him.

It was heavier than its size suggested. Someone had coated it in the anti-theft paint that had been popular for the past two years—which meant it wasn't too old to be recoverable—but on one side he felt an indentation, as if someone had pierced the cover with a fingernail.

It was all too easy to picture the previous owner holding this in a death grip in their final moments.

A sense of inevitable dread settled over him. It had been a mistake accepting the Lethe's offer. A mistake to be found on their radar at all. If he couldn't untangle himself—quickly—he would undoubtedly meet the same fate as the datcube's luckless owner.

"Have you considered the possibility that the information is corrupted?" Long asked. "I can guess which experts you would speak to, and who would recommend me, and there's very little I could do that they wouldn't have. There's no point in wasting your time if the data isn't salvageable."

Sonya shrugged. "I give it a twelve percent chance of being corrupted. It might be a keyed cypher, but the balance of probability says it's most likely an encryption."

"And the data?"

"Time sensitive only because of the employee's death."

A thin thread of hope appeared. "I realize it's tactless to ask, but is this datcube part of an ongoing investigation into that death? My clearance for several of my projects requires me to steer clear of the Jhandarmi and all local constabulary." Please say yes.

Sonya gave him another calculated smile, this one undoubtedly meant to make her look innocent and charming. "The employee died because of a burst heart. The coroner ruled it death of natural causes."

The coroners of Descent would rule a stab wound death by natural causes if the right people asked. It was a line of thought he didn't dare to follow. "The best I can offer is to look at the encryption. Without seeing it I can't tell you anything more."

"Can you have a status report to me by the end of the week?" Sonya asked with a polite smile that said 'No' wasn't an acceptable answer.

Three days to unlock the datcube and analyze the contents was a tight timeline if he wanted to focus on his other work, but it was doable. He nodded. "A status report, but nothing more. Do you have a copy of the cube that I can take with me?"

Her lips slipped into an uncharacteristic grimace. "That is our only copy."

"Ah." He set it down on the desk between them. "That makes security problematic."

"Your lab is secure?" she asked.

"The research lab is, but the outer office is designed with client comfort in mind."

Sonya nodded in understanding. "The datcube will be sent by armed courier. Lethe can offer you the standard security fee for priority technology as well as a consultant fee." She twisted the screen on her desk he could see the numbers.

Standard fees, nothing that raised any red flags, although the whole affair seemed suspect.

"If you are able to decode the data, there will be a sizable bonus. Have you ever worked with Lethe before?"

"I've never had the pleasure." Just as he'd never had the pleasure of being burned alive before. It was one of those little life-threatening things he'd made sure to avoid.

She pulled a paper contract from her desk drawer. "This is our consulting contract. While working on this project, you are not considered a Lethe employee and will not receive shares, benefits, or protections from Lethe. You will be paid commensurate to your skill level, and at the rate agreed. The contract terminates automatically after six weeks, unless both parties agree to extend the contract. Before, during, and after this project you are forbidden from disclosing the focus of the project with anyone other than your Lethe contact. Do you have any questions?"

Long looked over the paperwork. "Do you have the work of the previous groups that tried to decrypt this cube?"

"Would it be useful?" Sonya tilted her head.

"Knowing what they tried and what failed will save me time." And it would tell him who she had trusted.

Another small frown. "The other experts said they didn't want to be influenced by other people's processes." There was a hit of censure in her tone.

"We all approach work differently," he said. "I will probably look at it before reviewing their notes, but I don't feel the need to reinvent the wheel. Appearing like a genius to the world usually involves standing on the backs of geniuses who came before. It's how I did the decryption that I published in university."

Sonya gave a small nod, but he could see that she'd deducted a few points from the imaginary tally. "In that case, I'll make their work available to you. The records and a machine to process it on will arrive tomorrow. It goes without saying that everything stored on the computer becomes the property of Lethe after the contract is over."

"Of course." He made a mental note to scrub the machine for spyware and keep it away from his work lab and notes when it arrived. Lethe hadn't made their empire by playing fair.

Sonya stood up. "Then all is in order."

Following her lead, he stood too.

She posed, probably trying to look seductive. "I look forward to working with you, Doctor Long."

"And I look forward to working with you." As much as he looked forward to being eaten alive by ant lions. It was a trap, and the only way to escape was to move forward. If he could get Sonya the information maybe—just maybe—he'd escape with his life.

Keep reading: grab your copy now from
www.inkprintpress.com/lianabrooks/
malik/change/

CPSIA information can be obtained
at www.ICGtesting.com
Printed in the USA
LVHW031058170622
721527LV00003B/259

9 781922 434494